Janet Lennon

ADVENTURE AT TWO RIVERS

Authorized Edition featuring the singing star
from the Lawrence Welk TV show

By BARLOW MEYERS

Illustrated by
AL ANDERSEN

WILDSIDE PRESS

SUDDENLY Janet was frightened, and more completely alone than she had ever been in her life. Lifting her small suitcase, she went to stand uncertainly in the doorway of the station . . . .

This year Mr. Lennon had decided his famous singing daughters should have separate vacations. Excitedly Janet chose her cousin's dude ranch. But what she found at her destination proved almost more of a challenge than she could handle . . . cousins who treated her as an unwelcome guest, a bankrupt ranch, fires in the night, a half-crazed old man who would stop at nothing to get what he wanted, and trouble and danger at every turn.

Only after a mysterious stranger arrived at the ranch did Janet and the Kaywins see a way out of their difficulties. Success and happiness were close at hand, but with them came a series of narrow escapes which endangered the lives of all. As Janet packed to go home she realized that her Adventure at Two Rivers would be one of the most memorable and thrilling experiences of her life.

Contents

1   *"Leave It to a Girl!"*

Janet Lennon sat with her nose pressed against the train window and watched Wyoming slide past. Mountains, buttes, strips of timber, ravines and gulches, all of these patched with open grazing land, fell behind the rapidly moving train. Now and then a fence began at the right of way and disappeared in the distance. The country was beautiful but it was incredibly empty and lonely; throughout the morning she had seen less than a dozen human beings.

Suddenly her throat filled and she pressed her face harder against the window, turning away so that the passengers would not see the unexpected tear that went sliding down her cheek.

"What am I crying about?" she asked herself as she dabbed furtively with a handkerchief. "Nobody made me come. I was the one who wanted to go to a dude ranch for the summer. If I could just see somebody living out here!"

As though in answer to her wish a man on a fine bay horse came into sight. In the moment before he was left behind, the train whistled, the horse reared, and then plunged about trying to run. The man saw her and waved his hat.

Janet was still squeezing her face into the window corner, trying to see him as long as possible, when the voice of the stewardess spoke behind her. "Jackson's the next stop, Janet. About fifteen minutes."

"They'll get Mutty . . . they'll get my dog off the train all right?" Janet asked anxiously.

The stewardess smiled. "Mutty will be there. Don't you worry."

Janet began getting her things together, the stewardess helping her. When she finished, she sat down bolt-upright on the edge of the seat, feeling a little frightened.

As though she sensed Janet's feeling, the stewardess sat down and began talking. "You'll have a wonderful time,

Janet. I lived on a ranch when I was little. Horses, cattle, scenery and everything."

At the moment Janet would have loved having the train reverse itself, but she made herself smile and nod. "I'll have a wonderful time."

"Jackson! Ja—a—ckson!" It was the conductor coming through. Janet rose and stood in the aisle with the other passengers. In a moment she would see Cousin Martha, and the summer would begin.

On the platform a moment later, Janet picked up her suitcase and moved out away from the crowd so that she could easily be found and stood looking about. Singly or in groups passengers were met and taken to waiting cars. In five minutes the platform was empty except for the baggage man pushing his flat cart of mail sacks and trunks up toward the waiting room. Wild yelping came from the midst of the stack, and Janet left her suitcase and went flying up the platform.

"That your dog, miss?" the baggage man asked as she reached inside the small crate and patted the deliriously eager, whining, small cocker spaniel within. She nodded, happy momentarily with some well-loved creature at hand. The family's plans had required either taking Mutty to a kennel for the summer or bringing him with her.

"Stay here, Mutty, until they come for us."

The baggage man peered at the dog. "Don't look like a mutt to me. Looks purebred."

"He is," Janet said proudly, "but I call him that anyhow."

She returned to her suitcase and stood looking about for several minutes. Still nobody came. All the cars had departed. The baggage man had disappeared inside the station. Mutty had ceased wailing.

Suddenly Janet was frightened, more completely alone than she had ever been in her life. Lifting her small suitcase, she went to stand uncertainly in the doorway of the station, looking up at the incredibly majestic, gaunt ridges of the Tetons already shutting off the late afternoon sun. They looked blue and cold, and they cast great shadows over the valley of Jackson Hole below them.

Inside the station a telegraph key was clicking. She set her suitcase on a bench and went to the ticket window.

"Has anyone come today asking for Janet Lennon?" she asked. Perhaps Cousin Martha had been in to meet an earlier train.

The ticket agent surveyed her without interest. "Janet

Lennon, you say? Now who would be looking, miss?"

"A Mr. or Mrs. Kaywin of Two Rivers Ranch."

"Kaywin? Two Rivers? Never heard of either. Anywhere close?"

"I . . . I don't know. It's a dude ranch."

The sour bespectacled face leaned forward to look her up and down through bifocals. "Now, really, miss, I know every dude ranch in this part of the country. There's no Two Rivers that I know anything about. Sure you aren't off at the wrong station?"

"My ticket says Jackson, Wyoming," Janet told him a little shakily. If he was trying to make her feel a typical dude asking stupid questions, he was succeeding.

The agent hesitated uneasily. Then, as though wanting to be rid of her and the problem, he gestured toward the seats. "Sit down and wait a while, miss. Maybe they'll come. A delay maybe."

Feeling helpless, Janet went to sit beside her suitcase. She waited an hour, going to the door now and then to look up the street, then return. Occasionally the sour-looking agent trotted through the waiting room, glancing at her hastily as though fearing she might stop him.

She wished desperately that she were back at home. She

wondered what everyone there was doing and then re-membered. Most of the Lennons were on separate vacations this year.

This situation had been Dad's decision, made at the close of the school year. The winter had been a heavy one with many school activities. The practice for the television pro-gram had taken a great deal of time for the four singing Lennon sisters. The girls never relaxed their practice, and during May there had been evidence that they were tired.

The first day after school closed, everybody had been sit-ting around the living room, and no one had found much to say. It was as though a vague cloud hung over the room. Once Mother, bent over mending, had glanced from one to another of them; she had looked a little puzzled.

"What shall we do with these girls, Dad?" she had asked suddenly.

Dad was quiet behind his newspaper for a moment. Then he laid it aside. "I've been thinking about that."

Every head turned toward him. Things happened when Dad thought about things.

"I think," Dad said, "that our singing daughters need separate vacations this year."

His eyes twinkled as everybody straightened in surprise.

Mother's lips twitched as she bent over her mending again. "Why?"

Janet realized that her mother already knew what his answer would be. The question was just her way of getting him to give the girls his reasons for separate vacations.

Dad's tone was deliberate. "I think everybody's rushed all year. Everyone's tired. I'm tired of the office. Mother's tired of those everlasting socks." He smiled as Mother tossed the pile of socks on the table in mock eagerness. "You girls have worked together so long I think a little separation would be good for you. Now where would you like to go, and what would you like to do for the summer?"

Momentarily the girls were speechless. It was like Dad to make up his mind like this, plan immediately; even so, they were surprised. He looked at Kathy, waiting for her answer.

"Ellen is down in Florida!" she exclaimed. Ellen was Kathy's chum, vacationing there for the summer.

"Scout camp . . . if I can still get in!" Peggy's wish tumbled out eagerly.

"See about it," Dad told her. "Dianne, what about you?"

Dianne thought a moment. "I think I'd like to visit Gran in Chicago."

Mother's eyes twinkled. "Grandma probably will bear up under that wish very nicely."

Dad's eyes had come to Janet now and he waited. She had been listening so hard to the others she had to stop now and think for herself.

"I'd like to visit a dude ranch."

"A dude ranch? That's a long way, Janet. To find a recommended one this late in the season . . . ."

Mother straightened. "I have a suggestion. You know Cousin Martha with whom I exchange letters every Christmas and birthday? She lives near Jackson, Wyoming, and last Christmas she wrote they were starting a dude ranch. She's always inviting us out. Says they are so far away they never see relatives any more."

"Oh, Dad, could I?"

He glanced at Janet, then frowned. "I don't know, Janet. I have to be in Birmingham for three weeks just when I'd need to get you out there. It's a long trip."

The girls came together as though they had received a cue to sing on television. "Yippy-i-addy-iay! Let her go, Dad! She's a big girl now. There're trains, airplanes, buses."

They drowned him out if he tried to speak. Finally,

laughing helplessly, he tossed his newspaper over his head, pulled it sacklike down around his neck, and felt his way out of the room while the Lennon sisters made a quartet behind him.

"Oh, once on the prairie I used to go riding,
Oh, once on the prairie I used to look gay—"

So with the stewardess on the train keeping an eye on her, and with Mutty, her dog, riding in a crate in the baggage car, Janet had just finished a two-day trip across the country to Jackson, Wyoming. Waiters had seen that she was well-fed; the stewardess had visited with her. Now they were all gone and she was alone in the waiting room of the depot in Jackson, Wyoming, and it looked as though she would stay alone.

Disconsolately she wondered what her distant cousins were like. Her mother had given her the letter that had completed arrangements with Cousin Martha, who had wanted Janet to come as a family friend instead of a paying guest.

Dad, however, had sent a check ahead. "Sounds like the Kaywins need cash," he had remarked.

Reading the letter more carefully now, Janet could see what he meant.

> This is our first venture into dude ranching. We do not yet have the accomodations some places have, but we think we can show Janet a fine summer. She will have her own horse, her own room, and can do as she pleases. Greg, our son, is just a year older than she is, and Patty, the baby, is looking forward to having a big sister for the summer.

Four cousins she had never seen and, she glanced around the empty waiting room, probably never would see. Janet's throat filled, and even though there was no one to see, she went to the window and looked up the street to hide her tears.

Then in the distance she heard a racket. Blinking to clear her vision, she saw a pickup truck coming down the street at a fast clip. As it turned into the parking lot next to the window, she saw that it was an ancient model which had obviously survived an accident. Its brakes shrieked to a stop, and she saw that the left-front fender wobbled loosely, its jagged edges barely clearing the tire. The left

door was crushed in, the window broken.

A boy slid across the seat, opened a door that screamed on its hinges, and hurried into the station. Janet was still studying the truck when she heard him stop behind her.

She turned. "You're Greg, aren't you?"

He was staring at her with blue, smoldering eyes above a lanky length, a vantage point from which he could look down upon her. His expression was grim, his mouth straight and tight. She knew immediately that he did not like her, that he had come prepared not to like her.

"I'm Greg," he told her shortly. "You're Janet Lennon, I suppose. Well, come on."

She was halfway out of the station behind him when she remembered her suitcase and ran back for it. He saw her lugging it and took it from her. "Sorry," he mumbled.

"There's a trunk, too," she told him as he dropped the suitcase in the back of the pickup.

"A trunk!" He gave her a look that wilted her. "You staying all summ—?" He stopped, compressing his lips to shut off the rest. "Where is it?"

She fumbled in her handbag for the ticket. "It's in the baggage department. I'll get it."

He held out his hand for the ticket. "Give."

"I'll get it myself," she told him and started down the walk along the station.

He caught her arm. "Give!"

Under other circumstances the demand might have sounded teasing or good-natured. In Greg's case, it was neither. If this was Cousin Greg with whom she would spend a summer, she wanted as little of him as he did of her. "Listen," she told him, "I've got my round-trip ticket and I can go home instead of with you."

For a moment she thought he was going to tell her to go ahead, and she wished he would so she could walk loftily back into the station and wait for the next train. Instead, he reached out and took the ticket from her. "Come on! If I didn't take you home, Mom. . . ."

They identified her baggage, and he lifted it to his shoulder just as she said, "And there's my dog."

"Your what?" he cried.

"My dog, Mutty."

"My gosh, you mean we've got to feed—?"

"I'll take care of Mutty," she told him tartly, and she headed for the spot near the door to the baggage room from which wild yelps were coming.

Greg had gone out with the trunk. Janet was dragging

the crate to the door when he returned and reached for it. "Keep your fingers back. He bites people who don't like me."

The little fawn cocker growled as Greg lifted the crate, then growled louder as Greg muttered.

"What did you say?" Janet asked him.

"I said you must have quite a crowd of lawsuits with a pooch like that." He dumped the crate roughly in the back of the truck. "The crowds your dog has bitten must look like a state fair mob."

Janet ignored the remark. "I need to stop at a grocery."

"A grocery? Why?"

"Never mind. A grocery." She held her head high as she climbed in after him. Once seated, she stared ahead of her while he started the noisy motor and moved out of the lot.

On the main street of Jackson he pulled up in front of a grocery and she went inside. Minutes later she followed an aproned boy out and waited as he dropped a case of dog food in the truck while Mutty raved at him.

Janet stepped into the cab and settled herself. "There! Now you won't have to feed him!"

Greg took time to give her one furious, baffled look. "Leave it to a girl!"

2 *Unwanted Guest*

The truck rattled out of town, left-front fender banging. The pickup shook in every seam and joining. Even had Janet wished to talk, conversation would have been impossible. Greg sat stiffly at the wheel, his mouth grim and tense, his gaze glued to the road ahead as though she were not even present.

They went over a bump and Janet bounced. As she came down, she heard the case of dog food land hard, then her suitcases, and finally Mutty's crate. The dog gave a yelp of distress.

"Please don't drive so fast," Janet begged. "You'll hurt—"

"Hurt your mutt, I suppose!" he told her coldly. "That

would be a shame, wouldn't it? I can tell you this: If he can't stand being bumped in a crate, he isn't going to stand this country long, or you either!"

For the first time since they had left Jackson, he looked at her, his blue-eyed gimlet gaze taking her in as though she were a fly climbing a newly washed wall.

"I don't know why I'm so unpopular," she told him, "but I can tell you one thing. Mutty and I will be here as long as you will. It's a promise."

Greg shrugged. "Too bad."

Squelched, Janet dropped back into silence and tried to watch the scenery. The shadows had deepened now, the great peaks leaving the lower world in darkness while sunlight still shone like a nimbus over their tops. Greg turned on the headlights, and she watched them slicing their way through the timber lining the road.

Suddenly an animal dashed across the highway, and Janet straightened and pointed. "Oh, look!"

She had only time to see a beautiful antlered head, a body clearing the road in one magnificent leap, a white tail lifting like an upward pointing arrow, and the creature was gone.

"A white-tailed buck," Greg said. "They're beauties."

She glanced at him, seeing the dash light reflecting features for the moment warmed with pleasure. In that instant, she liked him. "Are there many here?" she asked.

"Thousands." He glanced in her direction, his eyes shining with enthusiasm. Then, as though he remembered who she was, his expression chilled again and he faced forward just as the front end of the truck began bumping and lurching sideways.

Thrown sharply against the door, Janet was conscious that the truck was veering to the left off the road, that Greg was desperately trying to stop it. She pulled herself upright just as he managed the feat, and staring in fright, she saw the headlights boring the darkness over an embankment that fell straight down.

"You—you all right?" Greg asked the question with his eyes looking out at the drop they had almost gone over. He still had one foot on the brake, but he released a hand from the steering wheel now and pulled the emergency brake.

"I'm all right," Janet told him shakily. "What happened?"

"I—I don't know. I had a smashup coming into town. An old man didn't stop at the main highway, just drove on and I hit him. I couldn't help it. Must have hurt the front wheel."

The dash light showed Janet that his hands shook a little. His voice sounded tight and hoarse. If he had been wrecked, no wonder he had been irritable and nervous when he came for her.

He opened the door and stepped out. "Hand me that flashlight in the glove drawer, please."

Janet found it, handed it out to him, and followed. He was shining the beam on the left-front wheel, lying half over on its side. By the reflected light Janet saw Greg run his hand through his hair. His face looked older than the fourteen she had been told he was.

"That crash cracked the axle probably. Anyhow, it means we walk the rest of the way home."

"How far is it?"

"About five miles." Greg stood about uncertainly for a couple moments. "I'll have to come get the truck tomorrow. We'd better start."

"What about my trunk?"

"Oh, I forgot. Your trunk and your suitcase, *and* your mutt, *and* your dog food!"

A quick retort rose to Janet's lips, but she smothered it.

"Give me the flashlight. Have you a screw driver I can pry with?"

Without comment Greg found the screw driver, and while Janet shone the beam of the flashlight on Mutty's crate, he pried it open with the cocker giving off warning growls. Released, however, the dog leaped about both of them, wriggling with wild delight. Greg ignored him while he stowed Janet's small trunk and the case of dog food in the cab of the truck and locked the doors.

He lifted Janet's suitcase to his shoulder. "Let's start."

Within half a mile they left the highway and followed a narrow dirt road that Janet could see dimly. The walking was rough and Greg was just a dim shadow ahead, but by staying exactly behind him, her feet kept the track without too much trouble except when Mutty, absorbed and joyous over new smells and surroundings, came dashing back continually to tangle himself in their feet.

Once he went wildly dashing after something, ki-yiing through the bushes, only to return moments later whimpering. Janet gathered him up. "Stay here, Mutty. Something will get you."

Balancing the suitcase on his shoulder and never breaking his stride, Greg remarked, "That would be a terrific loss."

Again Janet smothered a retort. In an attempt to change the subject, she asked a question. "Couldn't Cousin Martha come to the train?"

The moment the question was out, she had the sense of being critical, of having asked why Cousin Martha, instead of Greg, had not come.

Greg's answer, however, was immediate. "She had to stay with Dad. Said to tell you she was sorry. Dad broke his leg two weeks ago."

"I'm sorry. How did it happen?"

"Jacking up a tractor axle. The jack gave way and hit him in the shin. Mom took care of him at home."

No five miles had ever been as long as this, Janet thought. The road was rough now and overgrown. Rocks turned her ankles, and brush and sticks scratched her legs. She had another throat-choking moment of wishing she were with her family, wherever they were, but she remembered her remark to Greg that she would be here as long as he would, and she braced herself and trudged on after that rapidly striding figure. There probably would be no better time than this to prove the remark.

Finally, when she thought she could not walk another city block, she heard the distant baying of a dog.

House lights glimmered through the trees ahead. A horse nickered. Then a black-and-white shape rushed Mutty, whom she had put down a mile back, and she was surrounded with yelping, fighting turmoil. Mutty dashed between her legs for safety, and Janet fell hard.

"Tramp! Cut it out!" Greg shouted.

Shakily Janet climbed to her feet and gathered up her dog, who, from the safety of her arms, began growling and snarling at the big black-and-white shepherd.

Then a screen door opened and a woman holding a lamp stepped out on the porch. "Greg?"

"It's me, Mom."

"But why are you so late? Where's Janet? Oh, there you are, Janet."

The woman set the lamp on a table on the porch and came to the steps with hands outstretched. To Janet, dead weary, her legs shaking, she seemed the only sound thing in the whole night. She dropped Mutty and took the woman's big warm hands.

For a moment the bright lamplight of the big kitchen blinded her, but as her sight cleared she saw the table spread for supper, the big kitchen range giving off warmth, the tall thin man in a rocker on the other side of the room with his leg in a cast and supported on a straight chair. At his feet a little girl of about four sat on a stool and stared solemnly at Janet.

Janet let out a tired sigh she could not suppress and sank into the chair Martha turned for her. She gave the woman a feeble smile. She ached in every bone and muscle.

"My word!" Martha cried. "The child's done in. What happened, Greg?"

Greg, too, had dropped into a chair. "Give me time, Mom! You know that intersection just on the edge of Jackson where the road crosses the main highway? I hit a car there."

"You hit—oh, Greg, no!" Martha had been pouring water into a basin from the tea kettle on the stove, and she dropped the basin on the bench at the side of the room and sank down into a chair.

"You hit him or did he hit you?" The question came from the man in the rocker. That would be Jeff, Martha's husband, and his voice was so filled with weary resignation that Janet could not keep from turning to look at him. Obviously a collision, even one in which nobody was hurt, was a disaster of no mean proportions.

For a moment silence reigned with everybody staring at

Greg, who sat with his head down. "I hit him, I guess."

Again the hoarse, weary voice from the rocker. "Mean you don't know?"

"I hit him, but he drove onto the hard road without stopping. I had just turned that bend before you come to that intersection and I didn't see him in time and couldn't stop."

The silence that followed drew out unhappily. "What about the truck?" Martha asked.

"The left side is stove in, the glass smashed, the door jammed so it won't open. Then on the way home, the left-front wheel fell off, and we walked the rest of the way."

Again that unhappy silence. Greg's head dropped in frustration, his lips tight. Then he lifted his head and spoke explosively. "I'm sorry. I simply couldn't miss him. Maybe it's no excuse, but he didn't stop. I know we can't afford it!"

Greg stopped immediately, but not before Janet had caught the warning look Martha gave him, the almost imperceptible movement of her head toward her husband.

"We'll talk about it later," Martha said quickly, too quickly. "I'll bet you're starved, Janet, and worn-out, too. What an introduction to a dude ranch! Here, let's get you washed up, and you can sit down to some food right away."

Martha picked up the basin she had dropped, filled it with hot water, and handed Janet soap and a towel. "Wash up here, honey."

Janet caught the idea immediately. There was no bathroom in this house. By the time she had finished washing her face and scratched hands, Martha had food on the table and they all sat down, with Jeff taking his meals off a big tray across the arms of his rocker.

Had it not been for Martha's flow of conversation, questions about the family, where this was and that, Janet could not have kept awake during the meal. The evening had turned chilly, and the heat from the big stove now made her incredibly sleepy. Every muscle cried out for rest. The food was wonderful and bountiful, but Janet could hardly do it justice, and she did not know what she ate.

The moment the meal was through, Martha rose; she put her arm around Janet and led her toward a stairway that rose off the kitchen. "Now, honey, you come to bed. We'll get acquainted tomorrow. Greg, bring her suitcase."

Greg reached the foot of the stairway before she and Martha did, and he turned there to face them. Janet saw his throat muscles work as he swallowed hard. "Mom,

Dad, I didn't tell you all of it. You didn't ask me whom I hit. It . . . it was Old Man Dorrity."

Martha's hand on Janet's shoulder tightened convulsively. Janet glanced up to see Martha's lips open and close wordlessly. "Oh, no!" she whispered then.

The voice from the rocker spoke. "Well, that ties it."

"But, Mom, he was the one who was wrong. He ran the stop sign. I had the right of way."

"I know, Greg." Martha's voice sounded a little choked. "It's just . . . well, you know how it is."

Greg's glance went to his shoes and stayed there. "I know."

Silently the three of them went upstairs. Greg dropped her suitcase on the bed in a pleasant, old-fashioned room with an antique bed, and quaint red-ruffled curtains at the window. He went out without a word and again Janet had that feeling of resentment she had felt earlier.

Janet roused herself. "This Old Man Dorrity, is he so bad?"

Martha let out a long breath, a breath that seemed a little shaky. She went across the room to turn up the wick of the lamp that had been burning in the room when they entered. "I'd rather it had been anybody else in the world!"

She turned to Janet and managed a smile. "Sleep late in the morning, honey, and we'll show you around then."

When she had gone out, Janet opened her suitcase and got immediately ready for bed. She had just slipped between the sheets when she heard a sound from the distance, a long, drawn-out chopping yodel, as though the creature that made it breathed both in and out as he made the cry.

"I've probably heard my first coyote," she told herself.

Greg's face came to her mind before she dropped off. Why did he resent her? Jeff, too, did not favor her presence. She had a lot to find out about these distant relatives.

Then her eyelids closed down and she knew nothing more until morning.

3 *Sawdust for a Greenhorn*

The sun was high when Janet awakened the next morning. For several minutes she lay where she was, the events of the night before, with all their details that she had been too weary to notice then, seeping into her mind.

She could understand the Kaywins being upset over the collision, but Martha and Jeff had been almost in despair. There had been Martha's look of shock when Greg had finally told her whom he had hit. There had been Jeff's morose, "That ties it!"

Her glance slowly covered the bedroom. The smell of new wallpaper and paste still lingered. The red-ruffled curtains at the two windows were fresh and new-looking. A big old-fashioned wardrobe stood in one corner, and a pitcher and bowl waited on a washstand on the other side of the room. Home-braided throw rugs were on the floor. Janet sensed that this room had been readied for her coming.

From a distance she heard a creaking and rattling that came steadily closer. She sat up on the side of the bed and peered out the window. A team was towing the truck into the yard. Even towed by horses, the truck rattled almost as much as it had last night. Greg was handling the team and another man was in the truck guiding and braking.

By the time they had parked the truck on the far side of the yard near the old hay barn that apparently served also as a garage, Janet was dressing. Martha, her hands dusty with flour, was rolling out pie dough as Janet came into the kitchen. Jeff sat in his rocker as though he had never moved all night. He gave her the merest nod when she walked in, then returned to staring out the window.

"Well, Janet, how did you sleep?" Martha's smile was as warm and friendly as it had been last night.

"I don't remember."

Martha laughed. Dusting off her hands, she turned to the stove, lifted a lid and threw a chunk of wood into its flaming maw. "Bacon and eggs for breakfast?"

"I never eat a big breakfast," Janet told her. "Toast maybe, and—"

Martha poured a glass of orange juice from a pitcher she took from an old-fashioned icebox and handed the glass to Janet. "You'll eat out here. Everybody in Wyoming does. With all the things you'll do this summer, you won't last unless you do."

"Umphh." The sound came before Janet had time to answer Martha and was almost too low to be heard, but it was also too indignant to be missed. The grunt could have come only from Jeff, who was still staring out the window as though he had not even heard them.

To make conversation Janet asked a question to which she had already heard the answer. "Did you get hurt, Cousin Jeff?"

"Yep."

When he paid her no further attention, Janet turned uncertainly to the plate of food Martha set before her while she gave details of Jeff's accident which Janet had heard the night before from Greg. "Don't mind Jeff. If there's anything that acts as though it's caged, it's a rancher who has to sit in a kitchen for weeks."

"If a man had plenty of cash to pay for—" Jeff started.

"Now, Jeff." Martha shushed him. "Let's go have a look at that truck, Janet."

Outside Greg was at the rear of the pickup, and he glanced over his shoulder as he saw them coming. Janet saw him hastily throw an old blanket across something in the truck and go quickly to the front where he bent over, unfastening the chain with which they had towed the truck.

Martha studied the broken axle. "Well, it's a thorough job," she remarked wryly. "Our family car had a flat when time came to go for you, and that's why Greg took the truck."

Martha walked around to the rear of the pickup and looked at the wheel which Greg had put there. "That's not hurt, anyhow. What on earth's this under the blanket?"

She pulled away the old bed quilt and Janet saw the case of dog food she had bought yesterday. Martha turned to Greg. "Son, you didn't buy—"

"I bought it, Cousin Martha," Janet said quickly. "After all, I didn't ask if I could bring my dog Mutty, and you shouldn't have to feed him."

She heard the quick relieved breath Greg let out before he turned away toward the corral.

"My goodness, child, did you think we weren't glad to put up your dog?" Martha sputtered good-naturedly. "Let's look around, and then this afternoon Greg can take you riding."

At the corral Greg and the man who had been sitting in the truck were catching two horses, a black and a palomino. They tied the horses to the fence and immediately began firing a small forge standing near the open door of a shed.

Martha laid her hand on the neck of the palomino. "This is your horse, Janet. He's gentle. Ride him whenever you like. He'll always be in the corral or the pasture."

"He's beautiful!" Janet exclaimed. "What's his name?"

There was the least pause before Martha answered. "How about you naming him?"

"You mean he's never been named?"

"Never has," Martha replied briefly. "We think he's a nice horse. The black, Charcoal, is Greg's."

At that moment a hail, irritable and demanding, came from the window of the house. Martha sighed faintly, and turned away. "Jeff needs me. You look around, Janet."

Janet sat for a time on the top rail of the fence and made friends with the palomino. Patty had climbed up beside her. "What you going to name him, Jan—et?"

The color contrast in the horses was striking. They were charcoal and sawdust. "Sawdust!" Janet exclaimed. "That's what we'll call him, Patty."

"Mamma says I can't ride yet 'cause I'm only four," Patty prattled on, "but some day I'll ride Greg's horse." She leaned toward Janet and cupped her mouth in her hands. "Don't tell anybody, Jan—et. Greg and Mamma say I can't. But you wait and see."

Janet looked over at Charcoal. He was a gelding, restless and obviously spirited. He nipped at Greg when he passed and Greg slapped him lightly to make him behave.

"You'd better ride Sawdust, I think," Janet told Patty. "He's more our speed, don't you think?"

In her deliberate, positive fashion, Patty shook her head. "No, Jan—et. Some day I'm going to ride Charcoal." Her eyes, blue like Martha's, were determined. Her head, dark-haired like her father's, bobbed.

The forge was heated now, and Chuck, whom Janet surmised was the hired man, came over with four iron shoes which he held to Sawdust's hoofs, one at a time, to check for size.

"Gonna hold him for me?" he asked with a grin. He

was a short dark man with white teeth and a teasing expression. "Ever ridden much?"

Janet nodded and took the palomino's halter. "I've ridden a little, but we live quite a ways from a stable, so we don't get out to ride very often. I don't know much about horses really."

She stood stroking Sawdust's neck while Chuck heated and hammered the iron shoes into shape. With Greg nearby, she was not going to profess much horse knowledge, but she had enough to know that Sawdust was a good horse, although not young. The raised veins in head and neck showed age, and his rather rough coat and mane showed lack of care. She talked to him steadily in a low tone while Chuck worked, and Sawdust nudged her for attention every time she stopped running her hand down his neck even briefly. Obviously he was enjoying petting he had not had for some time. She glanced over at Charcoal, sleek and curried, black and shining. Again she came to the conclusion that Sawdust had come to Two Rivers only recently.

Finally Chuck dropped the last hoof and flexed his back. "Thank you, young lady. You have a hand with horses."

Janet turned toward Charcoal. "Shall I hold . . . ?"

Greg had forestalled the move. Already he had the rest-

less gelding out in the middle of the lot and was holding him himself, away from the fence. The move compelled Chuck to shift all his tools, and Janet recognized Greg's action as designed to keep her from touching Charcoal.

She climbed down from the fence. "Let's take a walk, Patty."

Together they skirted a wheat field just behind the corral and strolled to the opposite side where it bordered a strip of timber. While Patty constructed a playhouse under a bush, Janet climbed to the seat of an abandoned mower and studied Two Rivers in the distance.

The house was low, sprawling, old but pleasant. Set against the band of timber through which she and Greg had walked last night, it stood out sharply even though it lacked paint. The barn was of logs weathered by time, but sturdy. An ancient hay barn, its roof sagging, served also as a garage. Certainly it was not a dude ranch as Janet had thought of one, but for view one could not have asked for more. To the west the Tetons raised their splendid peaks, and to the east spread the low hills and knolls that made the real ranch country of Jackson Hole. A pasture came almost to the ranch yard and she could see cattle in the distance. Behind her, too, was timber, and a narrow wagon trail skirted its edge and led up along a narrow grassy valley to the north.

A bell sounded from the house and across the quarter mile of distance she saw Martha standing in the yard pulling the rope on the bell she had seen on a post there.

"Dinner, Jan—et. Come on. Run!"

Patty was not deliberate on footwork and Janet had all she could do to pace the child to the house. Both were gasping when they entered the kitchen.

"What can I do, Cousin Martha?" The table was set and Martha was at the stove, red-faced from the heat.

She gave Janet her hearty smile, although she looked hurried and harried. "Just call me Martha, honey. It's easier. That Cousin business could get old before summer's end. I'm about done here. I always ring the men in a little before I'm ready, so the food doesn't get cold. This is your vacation, so don't try to work. Just enjoy yourself."

Martha's tone was friendly but firm, and Janet retired with Patty to bounce a ball on the porch. The bumping of the ball and Patty's shrieks of delight at having a playmate did not prevent Janet from hearing an exchange of conversation in the kitchen.

"Better let her help, Martha. Dishes won't hurt her. Bet

she takes her turn at home." This was from Jeff.

"Doubtless she does, Jeff, but at home she isn't paying for a vacation summer. She isn't supposed to work out her board and room, you know." Her voice had hushed at the end and Martha began rattling dishes furiously. Then the men were in and washing up for dinner.

The meal over, Janet went outside to take pictures of Mutty, who had made his peace with Tramp. Both had been running through bushes and Mutty, deliriously happy, was wet, muddy, and covered with burrs.

Janet had finally posed him with Patty and was carefully aiming the camera when Greg's outraged tone reached her from the kitchen. "But, Mom, that top strand of fence in the south pasture is down. If the cattle climb it, we'll have trouble rounding them up. I can't take a girl jogging around the country when—"

Greg had said "girl" as though it were "jailbird." Janet heard Jeff's grumble of agreement, and then she heard Martha's firm tone. "You men, listen to me and for the last time! We have taken a summer guest. We have a responsibility for which we've been paid. It's true we had expected and hoped to have more guests, but since we haven't, we'll do all we can for this one."

"But, Mom . . . I haven't got time—"

Martha's tone rose past the murmur stage. "Greg, go get those horses ready and don't argue with me! And don't forget to lock up the dogs before you go."

Greg came out of the house as though he had been propelled. Without a glance at the girls he headed for the barn.

Patty threw the ball to Janet. "Know what? He doesn't want to take you riding."

"No," Janet replied ruefully. "He doesn't. I don't want to go either."

She turned toward the house to tell Martha she preferred not to ride, but at that moment Martha opened the door and handed Janet a wide hat. "Wear this, honey. Greg's taking you riding."

She returned inside as Chuck came out. "Come on, pilgrim. I'll give you a lift to the saddle."

He hurried Janet along so there seemed no opportunity to back out. "What's a pilgrim?" she asked.

"A greenhorn," he grinned. "You're out of that class when you've fallen in a river, been pitched off a horse, and chased by a bear."

Sawdust was already ground-tied in the corral and ready.

Greg was saddling Charcoal with swift, hard motions. Before anyone could help her, Janet went to the palomino, pulled the reins around his neck, and put her foot in the stirrup. He was a tall horse and the rise to the saddle took effort, but she made herself go up with a long easy swing. No man was going to push her into the saddle.

"Hey, you been there before!" Chuck exclaimed. "Maybe you ain't such a pilgrim after all."

"There's still the river and the bear," she told him.

Chuck swung the corral gate open and she followed Greg out and down along the road past the wheat field. The boy's face was moody. His black horse pranced and swung sideways, but Greg handled him beautifully. Sawdust traveled quietly, and his gait was smooth. She felt pleased that he held his head well, even tugging against the bit a little as though he wished to look as fine as the black. Janet made no attempt at conversation, but for half an hour she followed, getting used to her horse, enjoying the scenery. If this was what Daddy had paid for, she would see that she got as much out of it as possible.

Beyond the wheat field Greg followed the narrow wagon trail that led up the long valley to the north and finally led alongside a barbed-wire fence skirting a pasture with an ancient log cabin that lay perhaps a city block from the road.

"Who lives there?" Janet broke the silence for the first time.

"Old Man Dorrity."

"Oh, that man you hit!"

As though he relished no conversation on the subject, Greg touched his heels to Charcoal and took off up the road. Sawdust followed and Janet forgot the cabin and concentrated on riding.

Five minutes later Greg pulled up on the bank of a fifty-foot-wide stream brawling its blue-and-white way down out of the mountains over a rock-strewn bottom.

For the first time Greg spoke voluntarily. "Pacific Creek." He turned in his saddle and pointed to the barbed-wire fence that had bordered the trail. The strands of fence on their posts squared away perhaps thirty feet before the creek to allow travelers to reach the point where the bank dropped to the ford. "I'd better warn you," Greg told her, "never to cross that barbed-wire fence. Dorrity doesn't like trespassers, and it's only public opinion around here that makes him let people use this crossing. Actually it's on his land, and he had trouble with a few people before he gave up and refenced his land right here."

"Why didn't he want people to use it?" Janet asked.

Greg shrugged. "He's that kind. What's mine is mine and you let it alone. Out here stream crossings are touchy subjects. Our neighbor, Hayward of the Lazy O, gave him a lot of trouble about it, so now we all use it, but we don't stick around on it, and we don't cross his line."

Done with explanation, Greg turned Charcoal and dropped him down the steep bank to the water. Sawdust followed without a pause, and the two horses, moving slowly, their feet feeling for rocks, went over, the water rising beyond the stirrups so their riders pulled their feet up to stay dry.

Then Greg was going up the other side with Charcoal plunging. He disappeared over the top and as Sawdust came out of the water Janet loosened the reins, and then clung frantically as the palomino, too, went up in a series of bounds that almost slipped her out of the saddle.

"Wait!" she cried. Then she kicked Sawdust. She would not be left behind by Greg Kaywin!

Greg had disappeared among the clumps of bushes ahead, but she could hear the hammer of hoofs ahead. The ground was flat here, and Sawdust, galloping at a fast clip, rounded bushes and aspen thickets so closely that Janet was almost raked from the saddle. Then the undergrowth cleared and she saw Greg ahead. Clinging to the horn, she kicked Sawdust again and steadied herself in the saddle. The old horse gave out with a burst of speed that almost closed the gap, and she caught up with Greg at the point where the wide flat ended at the foot of a steep trail that led up to a sign. PRIMITIVE TERRITORY, it said. NO CARS PERMITTED BEYOND THIS POINT.

4 *Dogs, Guns, and Danger*

Having kept her seat in the saddle successfully, Janet felt like yielding a point. If she and Greg must share the same ranch for the summer, there was little reason to be enemies.

"Greg, what is primitive territory?"

"It's land the Government holds in reserve."

"For what?"

"Tourists." Greg's tone held a faint edge of scorn. "Timber. It's also a game preserve, and Uncle Sam's method of keeping the country the way it was in old times. The only roads in here are narrow trails, and you come in either walking or on horseback."

Already the timber had closed around them. Voluntarily the horses dropped to a walk. Everything seemed hushed and quiet, the creak of saddle leather, the padded footfalls of the horses the only sounds. Flowers, lavish in color, were everywhere.

"It's . . . it's so green," Janet said. Her voice broke into the silence much too loudly, and she hushed it before she reached the end of the short sentence.

Greg's voice had dropped to the same hushed note as her own when he replied. "There's lots of water in Jackson Hole. Lakes and streams that give the place plenty of color."

They had traveled a silent mile when Janet saw a lake glimmering through the green that surrounded them. Very quietly Greg held up his hand to stop them. "You think it's quiet in here, but listen."

For a moment Janet heard nothing but a scolding jay. Then as he flew away, she heard a murmuring sound, faintly staccato, but muted, a reassuring, contented sound, stopping and starting.

She was struggling to place the sound that came from the lake ahead, and finally she came up with the answer. "It's a duck. But I never heard one sound like that."

Greg turned in the saddle, and for the first time she had a feeling she saw the real Greg. His morose expression and resentment had vanished from a face now serene and listening. He was in a region he loved, and he was intent on absorbing all that was there. He was happy and satisfied.

"It's a drake, and the hen is nesting close. He guards and entertains her while she hatches the eggs."

They sat their horses, taking in the sounds. Janet did not speak for fear of reminding Greg that she was there, for then he might return to the self she had seen before. The scene, too, might change.

She was right. Sound broke out behind them and came closer, the bass barking of Tramp, the shepherd, and the shriller more excited yelping of Mutty. Other sounds then broke everywhere. A band of crows flew away cawing loudly. Blue jays screamed.

Greg, his face darkening with irritation, looked beyond her until the dogs broke through and came panting happily up beside the horses. "Those mutts got out," he growled. "Oh, well!"

Scowling, he turned back in the saddle and rode on past the lake where no ducks either showed or sounded now. The next hour was noisy, with Tramp scouting the undergrowth everywhere and Mutty yelping and panting in determined desperation to keep the pace.

As though he had made up his mind to give Janet her

money's worth, Greg rode places Janet had not known a horse could go. She knew enough to give Sawdust his head, but sometimes she was frightened.

Once Greg came to the edge of a steeply slanting bluff. He paused to study the descent briefly. "Surely," Janet thought, "he isn't thinking of riding down that."

"Deer have been going down there," Greg remarked casually, "and where deer go horses can go." With that he rode Charcoal off over the edge.

Janet's mouth opened to cry out a refusal to follow him. Then she shut it firmly. This was the third opportunity Greg had given her to make good her boast that she would still be around, no matter what came up. She shut her eyes tight and clung to the saddle horn as Sawdust lowered himself carefully over the edge. Then, fascinated, she had to watch him go down with expert care, step by careful step, his weight always held back a little until he knew the footing would hold.

Several feet from the bottom Charcoal suddenly leaped out onto the level, and Greg rode away as though she were not present. Sawdust also leaped and almost left Janet in mid-air. Janet, righting herself in the saddle, looked behind and up at the course they had come and shuddered. She stared furiously then at Greg's back. There was a certain set to his head and shoulders, a consciousness of what he had done and of her reaction to it. He had deliberately intended to scare her.

For another hour she followed him along the narrow trails, surmising that he was gradually circling around to their point of entrance to this country. Once far ahead, she heard the thunder of falling water and Greg led them up past a small, beautiful waterfall that seemed to plunge out of the trees and drop for thirty feet into a fern-lined chasm and roar away.

Greg paused to look down at it, his face again a study in pleased relaxation. "Not many even know it's here."

She sensed his feeling of secret pride and felt a little proud herself. This was where Greg came sometimes, and he had shown it to her.

Then suddenly they were back where they had come in, and Greg was riding fast across Cottonwood Flat toward Pacific Creek, with the dogs racing and barking alongside the horses. Easier now in the saddle, Janet could watch Mutty's frantic efforts to keep the pace, his joy at all this freedom and country at his disposal. He had never had either before.

Once across Pacific Creek they walked the horses and Janet had time to notice that a quarter of a mile across a grassy overgrown pasture, enclosed by the barbed wire Greg had warned her never to cross, was a dilapidated log cabin flanked by a couple small outhouses opening, as nearly as she could make out at this distance, into fenced chicken yards.

"Is that the house of the Old Man Dorrity that you hit yesterday?" Janet asked.

Greg turned in his saddle to speak to the dogs, urging them in close to the horses. "That's the one. Come on, pups!"

At that moment a cottontail rabbit leaped up almost under Charcoal's hoofs and went bouncing under the old barbed-wire fence that enclosed the pasture. With wild ki-yiing Mutty took after him, and Tramp followed.

"Tramp!" Greg yelled. "Come back here! Oh, gosh!"

Greg had jumped from his horse and was rolling under the fence in a second.

"What's wrong?" Janet cried. "They can't catch that rabbit anyhow, Greg!"

Greg was already out in the pasture and now Janet saw what had caused his alarm. With a roar of wrath an old man with a gun in his hand had burst out of the cabin and was running across the overgrown yard to intercept the dogs. Once clear of the broken fence, he raised his gun and aimed.

Janet slid off Sawdust. "Mutty! Mutty, come back!"

She felt her blouse catch on a barb as she rolled under the bottom wire of the fence. Then she was running across the pasture as the gun fired. The dogs were so intent that they never paused but continued course on the rabbit which was running within a hundred feet of Old Man Dorrity. Greg was yelling at them and running, and now Janet saw the old man raise the gun again, taking aim at the dogs.

Then she stopped in horror. "Oh, Greg! Don't!"

Greg had changed course and was running directly at the man. He reached him a split second before he pulled the trigger and struck the gun barrel up so that the shot went wild. The rabbit, blocked by a ledge of rock that flanked the house on the far side, turned at right angles, dashed through the yard, and disappeared.

Paralyzed with fear, Janet watched the man and boy struggle for the gun. Then with a savage wrench the old man flung Greg aside, grabbed the gun by the barrel and swung it over his head.

"Greg, get out of the way! Run!" Janet screamed. She had forgotten the dogs. The malevolent face with its scraggly beard and yellow teeth showing through, the wild eyes . . . the whole picture seemed something from another, horrible world.

Then Greg was running. "Get going!" he panted. "Run!"

Together they sprinted for the fence, hearing Dorrity panting along behind them. "I've told ye afore—an' I'll tell —ye agin! Keep offen—my propity!"

She had never run so fast and so desperately in her life. Greg flung himself under one section of wire, and she followed, feeling the wicked barbs tear at her shirt again. Shakily she got to her feet and reached her horse before she turned.

Greg was standing facing the fence now. "We're not on your property now," he told Dorrity quietly. "We just wanted to get the dogs off."

"Ye better stay off, too!" Dorrity told them. He turned and stalked back toward his house, a rapidly moving, bent figure of vengeance. Somewhere in the distance the dogs were still barking.

Janet let out a long, shaky breath and collected strength

enough to pull herself to the saddle. "No wonder you're scared of him!"

Greg wheeled on her. "I am *not* scared of him! I've got orders, that's all. Never go on his place. Never cross his path if it can be helped. And what happens? Our dogs chase a rabbit across his pasture. And yesterday? At this season tourists by the thousand in Jackson Hole, and who do I have to hit? Old Man Dorrity!"

"But who is he? I don't understand. I mean, is he crazy or something?"

Greg gave an exasperated sigh. "He's an old hermit and general trouble maker. Hates everybody and the Kaywins in particular. You should have heard him yesterday. He threatened to sue and all I'd done was dent his fender. Once a month he drives that old jalopy to town for groceries, and that has to be the day we collide. You should have heard him!"

"Let him sue," Janet said. "That's why you've got insurance."

"Yeah, but our insurance takes care of the other fellow, but not our own cars. We get it cheaper that way. Now this accident puts another heavy bill on the folks. It's *always* like that!"

"But why does he especially hate the Kaywins?" Janet asked.

"His reasons sound as unreasonable as anything else he does. About two months before he came to Jackson Hole the Government sold Dad and Mom twenty acres of land that had originally been part of the ranch he's got now. He's felt it should be returned to his tract."

"A gift, I suppose?" Janet inquired. "He sounds crazy."

Greg mounted now and rode on down the road. His shoulders had lost their defiance and slumped in a pose that made her think of his father in the rocker. "He'd like it as a gift, no doubt. About his being crazy, I don't know whether it's that or he's just peculiar."

Not knowing what more to say on the subject, Janet looked behind to see if the dogs were in sight.

"Greg, what about the dogs? They were in his back yard the last I knew. Will he kill them?"

"I doubt if he goes that far. Besides, the dogs probably chased the rabbit on out of the yard and are a couple miles away by now. They'll get home."

Janet wished she could feel as sure of all this as Greg seemed to be. She kept looking over her shoulder trying to sight the dogs.

Then her attention was taken by voices ahead. The sounds indicated a dozen people coming. A man on a big bay horse with a star and four white socks appeared around the bend. The high-headed bay shied at the sight of them, and the big man riding him brought him around with superb horsemanship. The man was not young, but he was handsome and smiling. His Western-style clothes, pearl-grippered and tailored, fitted him to perfection, and his wide hat had a band of silver conchas around the crown.

"Well, hello, Greg. Out for a ride?"

Greg nodded. Janet saw him swallow hard as he had the night he had told his parents of the accident. He would have gone by quickly, but the rider pulled his horse alongside. "How's your dad, Greg?"

"He's coming along all right." For a moment Greg hesitated until he saw the rider glance at Janet. "Mr. Hayward, meet Janet Lennon, our guest for the summer."

Janet could not help noticing the least hesitation in Greg's manner. Greg had tried to avoid introducing her.

Mr. Hayward lifted his hat and smiled. "Enjoying Jackson Hole, young lady? Meet our guests." One after another, he called off the names of the eleven people who had gathered around them. They were smiling and friendly, and they came from all over the country. Through with his introductions, Hayward touched the bay with his heels. "Got to get on. Bring your guest down, Greg. We'll be glad to see you."

She and Greg rode for a city block before either spoke. Greg's face again was moody and he did not look in her direction.

"Were they from a dude ranch?" she asked finally.

Greg nodded, and she saw the corner of his lip twitch unhappily. Janet wished she had not asked. Those people had come from a real dude ranch, with many guests. She was the only guest Two Rivers had been able to get for the summer.

When they reached home, Martha came out into the yard. "Did you enjoy your ride, Janet?"

Janet's mouth was open to tell her the events of the afternoon, but from the corner of her eye she sensed that Greg had sent a glance her way. "I loved the ride," she answered. "I had a wonderful time, and I liked Sawdust, too."

"My goodness, what happened?" Martha exclaimed. She fingered Janet's torn blouse.

"I caught it on the fence," Janet explained.

At nine o'clock that night no dogs had appeared. Martha had gotten food ready for them and called without results. Janet could not keep her mind on the book she was reading. Was Mutty locked up? Perhaps dead?

Finally she could stand it no longer. Martha was in the kitchen, and Janet told her the events of the afternoon. "Do you think the dogs will come back, Martha?"

Martha looked pained. "Oh, dear! Dorrity again! We just can't seem to keep from running foul of that man. It was my fault that the dogs got out. I left the pen gate open a minute. I don't think, though, that he'd really hurt them. Sometimes Tramp goes away for a day or two. They'll probably be home in the morning."

Janet did not feel much reassured. "I guess I'll go up to bed."

Upstairs she got out her pen and note paper.

Dear Mother and Daddy, I am afraid I am going to be sorry I wanted to come to a dude ranch. I have lost Mutty. Greg had an accident coming to town to get me, and I am afraid he doesn't like me at all. We had to walk home in the dark, and we got into trouble with an old man named Dorrity.

Janet stopped and reread what she had penned. Somehow

it sounded very sorry-for-yourself. Suddenly she felt terribly sleepy. She got ready for bed and climbed in, then sat up listening in the dark, hoping to hear dogs barking. Once she thought she heard them far away, but she could not be sure. She slid under the covers and lay back, letting tears wet the pillow. She wanted to sob but would not let herself. She managed to go to sleep without allowing one sob to escape.

5 *The Rescuers*

Daylight was barely evident when Janet awakened from a restless night during which she had repeatedly roused to listen for dogs. Downstairs she heard Martha's voice, then Greg's, and the sound of a chair being pulled across the floor. Stove lids rattled, the porch door banged. Chuck Malone moved through the mist toward the barn. The Kaywins were readying themselves for the day.

Janet dressed hurriedly, ran a comb through her hair and straightened her bangs. She was pulling a sweater on when she noticed the letter she had written her family last night. Read by morning light, it sounded more sorrowful than ever. She tore it to bits and dropped it in the wastebasket, feeling that she had been childish. If she was old enough to take a vacation alone, she was old enough to handle whatever came out of it without complaining.

"Why, Janet! You're up too early!" Martha was slicing bacon at the table.

"I couldn't sleep any longer. Martha, did the dogs come home?"

"No." The short, clipped reply came from Greg whom she had not noticed leaning in the doorway staring outside. He did not turn to look at her or his mother, but Janet sensed that his uneasiness about the dogs was as great as her own.

Martha glanced from one to the other. "Don't worry about them, Janet. Tramp's probably showing Mutty all the sights of Jackson Hole."

Breakfast was on the table in half an hour, and Janet made herself eat heartily of bacon and eggs, biscuits and wild honey. She had something to do today. Afterward she wiped the breakfast dishes for Martha and tried to make conversation with Jeff. She had tried this ever since her arrival, but she was having no better luck than before. Apparently, for some reason Janet did not understand, he resented her presence here and he was not going to say any more than "yes" or "no" unless compelled to do so.

She gave up the attempt when the last dish was in the cupboard and went to sit on the porch steps. Greg had gone to the corral and she could hear him and Chuck talking, their voices clear in the morning air.

"I'll ride down and fix that south fence," Greg was saying. "What are you going to do today?"

"Got to get that mower fixed, ready to cut hay when the dew's off."

Within a few moments Greg rode out of the yard on Charcoal with a canvas sack of staples on the saddle horn and a roll of barbed wire over his arm. Shortly afterward Chuck, hammer and wrench in his hand, headed for the hay field.

Janet glanced at the sky. The sun was coming through now although the mist was still heavy. "Martha, I'm going for a ride."

Martha came to the door. "Oh. But, Janet, shouldn't you wait for someone to go with you? It's so easy to get lost in this country."

"I won't go that far—not up into primitive country where Greg took me yesterday or anything. I'll be careful. And I can saddle Sawdust, I think."

Sawdust had been left in his stall. Janet found the bridle

he had worn yesterday and managed to slip the bit between his teeth and the headstall over his ears. The saddle was a harder matter. It was heavy and twice she knocked off the blanket trying to heave the tree to his back. Fortunately Sawdust had patience and stood quietly for her awkward maneuvers.

Once she was mounted, however, he balked, refusing to go through the open gate of the corral. Yesterday he had had another horse to follow and he was not going to travel out alone today. Although he did not try to throw her, he backed and stalled, or simply stood while she hammered his sides with her heels. She could have wept with frustration.

Just when she was about to give up and put the horse back in his stall, Chuck Malone spoke behind her. "Here, work him over with this. That chap knows exactly what to do with pilgrims. You'll have to unlearn him. Try this. And yell at him at the same time."

"Oh, Chuck, thanks!" Janet took the two-foot willow switch he passed up to her, and in her anger she brought it down hard on Sawdust's rump and shouted at him. He almost went out from under her, and the next moment she was galloping out through the yard at full speed with

Martha running out on the porch calling after her.

"I'm going where Greg is," Janet called back.

Within a quarter of a mile, Sawdust dropped to a jog, but he kept wary ears turned back to her, and he started forward every time she lifted the switch.

By following the fence line that bordered the road, Janet finally saw Greg inside the cattle pasture, stringing a line of barbed wire along the top of a row of posts. She had now fulfilled her remark to Martha: she had gone where Greg was.

She turned off the road in the opposite direction and entered the unfenced timber. She glanced back once as Charcoal nickered. Greg had turned and was watching her. She waved and he gestured disinterestedly in return and went back to hammering staples.

The mist had thinned now, but Janet made a careful check on her position before losing herself in the forest entirely. She was not unmindful of what Martha had told her about disappearing tourists. She was south of Two Rivers, and the Dorrity ranch lay north, if that forty acres of spite and trouble could be called a ranch. Her purpose was to reach it without going back through or past Two Rivers, and that meant circling through the timber to the east. It also meant keeping her bearings.

The forest seemed to close around her. Grass, under-growth, and tree branches were mist-hung, and within minutes she was soaked to the skin. Looking behind her, she could see the trail Sawdust made knocking aside the wetness.

Her watch told her she had ridden for an hour before she saw the small open pasture, with the ancient log cabin, ahead of her through the trees. Suddenly she heard something. She pulled Sawdust to a halt and sat listening so hard she held her breath. A dog was yelping mournfully, and even through a quarter of a mile of distance she caught the sound of restless whining. Then she heard Mutty, his shrill bark shutting off suddenly after a sound like a report or a thud.

Hurriedly Janet slipped from the saddle and tied Sawdust to a tree. Then she was pushing her way as silently as possible through the timber toward Dorrity's cabin. Remembering the ledge of rock that rose behind his dwelling, she made her way toward it. Soaked with dew and brier-scratched, she found herself panting on top of it finally, where she could look directly down into the old man's back yard.

At first glance the place had a crumbling look of cluttered serenity. The leaning old cabin looked out on a back yard with tins cans showing through the weeds. The only sound and well-repaired part of the whole outlay was the double chicken yard, each with a small house at the back, and the whole surrounded by a high mesh fence. In one a dozen chickens were huddled along one side, their high silly heads turning one way and another as though they had just been startled. The other, at first glance, appeared empty.

Her glance roved to the house, and for the first time she saw Dorrity sitting in a battered rocker on an open porch facing the chicken yards. A bucket sat beside the rocker, and leaning against the other side of the rocker was a rifle. Dorrity himself, taking the morning air in a pair of ancient overalls and an old suit coat with a rent halfway up the back, looked as pleased as Janet had yet seen him. He watched the chicken yard closely . . . too closely.

Janet sank to her knees behind the screen of blackberry bushes that grew across the front of the ledge. "He's not killing time," she whispered aloud. "He's watching something."

Then a rock rolled down the ledge which she had climbed and she wheeled in fright, her first thought that she had allowed herself to be cornered by a bear.

Greg's head showed over the ledge. "What are you doing here?" he hissed.

Janet let out a gasp of relief. "You scared me! I'm watching Dorrity. I think he's got Tramp and Mutty in his chicken house."

Suddenly a shout, the thud of something on wood, a short hurt howl followed by Mutty's whine dropped both Janet and Greg down on their stomachs to peer through the bushes. They were just in time to see Tramp's white-tipped tail disappearing inside the door of the chicken house, and a rock bouncing away. Then Mutty showed in the doorway. Dorrity's hand dropped to the pail, lifted an egg-sized rock and hurled it. It passed forcibly through the screen wire and hit the door beside the little cocker's head and Mutty disappeared hastily inside, whining.

Furious, Janet leaped to her feet, her mouth opening to shout at Dorrity. Greg grabbed her arm and pulled her down. "Keep quiet! Do you think we're ever going to get those dogs away from Dorrity by shouting at him? Don't be crazy!"

Hastily Janet sank down, for Dorrity had apparently heard something. He had risen and was staring up at the ledge farther north than where they lay. Both Greg and she pulled back and lay flat, heads against the rock as his glance covered their spot and moved on.

"Let's get out of here and go where we can talk and plan something," Greg whispered.

They were at the foot of the ledge and two hundred feet from the cabin before they spoke again. "How did you find me?" Janet asked.

"Followed your trail through the dew," he replied in a low voice. "Got to watch out for dudes in this country."

His superior tone irked her, but she had no time to waste. "What are we going to do about the dogs?"

"I don't know," Greg said seriously. "Maybe tonight . . . ."

"Did you see that rifle in the corner?" Janet whispered hotly. "By tonight he'll have shot them."

Sudden barking broke out from the other side of the ledge. Again there was the shout, the thump of a rock.

"You're probably right," Greg said. "I think I'll just walk in there and ask him for the dogs."

Janet, aghast, was just as frightened for Greg as she had been provoked with him a moment before. "That old man would as soon shoot you as the dogs. You can't, you don't dare go in there, Greg! Not after yesterday!"

Greg got to his feet and started around the ledge. "We'll have to do something and do it now. I'll tell you what. I'll go in and try to decoy him out to the front, maybe chasing me off. You slip in and turn the dogs loose."

"Greg, it'll never work. We don't dare." Somehow Janet sensed that under his calm surface he was as scared as she was but was covering it up with bravado. "Listen! Let me go, and you turn the dogs loose. He probably won't hurt a girl."

"A girl won't bother him a bit—" Greg started to say. "Janet, come back here!"

Janet was off and running up toward the front of the house before he could catch her. She turned and waved him back, making a gesture to indicate that he should go around the ledge and be ready for whatever might happen. Greg made a frustrated gesture, shook his head and retreated.

Janet continued quietly until she stood beside the leaning front porch of the cabin. Now and then from the rear she heard Dorrity's diabolical chuckle and the thump of a hurled rock, but she continued waiting until sure that Greg had time to go around the ledge.

Finally, swallowing hard, she walked around the house. "Hello, Mr. Dorrity. I've come to talk to you about the dogs." She rushed on because she was afraid if she hesitated her voice would quaver. "I'm sorry they trespassed yesterday. We had them locked up but they got out. I promise it won't happen again."

She almost stuttered to the finish, for Dorrity had leaped to his feet, and seen this close he was a more fearsome sight than before. His hair had gone uncut for weeks, and his eyes alternately smoldered between half-closed lids, then blazed out in open fury.

"Young lady, if'n you think them pups go home until I've had a talk with your pappy, you're mistaken. You tell *him* to come talk! I don't waste time on sprouts!"

Obviously Dorrity did not know she was not a Kaywin. She chose not to inform him. "But Dad can't come. He's hurt."

"Cain't help that. I didn't hurt him. If he wants his dogs tell him to be here before tonight, or . . . ."

By now Mutty had recognized his mistress. He was pawing the fence and barking madly. Dorrity reached down and grabbed a rock which hit the fence wire, then struck Mutty a glancing but hard blow. He yelped in distress and

backed away, shaking his head. Dorrity reached for another rock, his yellow snags of teeth showing through his dirty beard.

"Oh, please don't!" Janet begged. "Don't hurt him!"

"Then git!" Dorrity snapped. "I don't like trespassers, dogs, or wimmen—an' you air two out of the three."

Janet's throat was thick with fear, but she remembered that she had snatched from Greg the task of decoying Dorrity out of his own yard. She was handling the job poorly. She would have to think of something.

"I . . . I'll go. But would you come down and open the gate for me? Yesterday I tore my blouse rolling under the wire." It was all she could think of for an excuse to get him away.

"You got in," he told her grimly. "Git out the same way!"

Suddenly Janet knew she was going to cry. She was so angry with herself for spoiling the plan. She dabbed at her eyes furiously. Abruptly Dorrity dropped a rock back in the pail and stepped off the porch. "Come on, gal, before yuh drown me! Git!"

He stumped around the corner of the house and once he'd started across the pasture, Janet ran ahead of him. Perhaps then he would not look back and see Greg.

Two-thirds of the way across the pasture a wild joyous yelping broke out and Mutty came flying after her. Janet broke into a run of sheer terror as Dorrity's hoarse roar of wrath sounded behind her. She had reached the fence and rolled under the wire before she dared to look back. Dorrity was back in his yard shaking his fists after Greg who was just disappearing in the timber at the foot of the ledge on the south.

She scrambled to her feet and started running down the road toward Two Rivers. "Hurry, Mutty." There was no need to urge the cocker. He was well ahead of her and headed for home.

Half a mile from Dorrity's lower fence line she met Greg riding Charcoal and leading Sawdust. She was gasping for breath as she climbed to the saddle. "Why—doesn't somebody *do* something about that old man?"

Greg grinned. "Any suggestions? He's a citizen who owns his land and doesn't like visitors. No law against it that I've heard about."

Greg was looking at her and suddenly he burst into laughter. "What's the matter?" Janet asked testily.

"Got a mirror?" Greg asked.

Janet looked down at herself. The leg of her blue jeans

was ripped from knee to ankle, and her shirt was grass-stained and covered with twigs. She put up a hand and could feel the same in her hair.

As though he recognized that she was in no mood for joking, Greg sobered. "Do you think the rest of us like living next to Dorrity? Especially, the Kaywins don't. Our land adjoins his, so we have more to stand than the others. It's an everyday problem to be sure none of our stock break down his old fences. Dad is sure that's the way we lost that prize herd bull a year ago."

"How was that?" Janet asked.

"The bull had apparently worked himself halfway through the fence, and he'd been dropped right there with a nice round hole in his head. Dad even went to Dorrity, and I can hear the old misfit yet. 'No, Mr. Kaywin, I never shot your bull. Here's my rifle. You can see it ain't even been fired.' He got it down off a closet shelf as though it had been up there for years. As if that proved anything! It was all nicely oiled. Come on, Janet. I got work to do at home."

The fast, exhilarating ride home, the relief at the rescue of the dogs smoothed Janet's anger and fear away. At the corral she was surprised to see that her wrist watch showed only nine thirty. It seemed she had been gone much longer, but then she remembered that it had been only six thirty when she rode out of the ranch yard. She brushed off her clothes, borrowed Greg's pocket comb, and washed her face at the horse trough, all in an effort to keep Martha from noticing anything wrong with her appearance.

Martha took one look at her. "My goodness, child, you certainly do wreck your clothes out here. You've torn your jeans and I'll bet the grass stains won't come out of that blouse. I told you those dogs would turn up by themselves."

6   *A Very Close Call*

Janet had arrived at Two Rivers in the middle of June and, for a change, the rest of the month went along more peacefully than the first two days had done. She played with Patty, and after discovering that Sawdust was agreeable to being ridden double, took the little girl with her on rides around the ranch. By now Martha had given in to Janet's doing a certain amount of work. In trying to estimate that amount, Janet tried to cut a line by giving bits of help here and there without getting Martha upset because she was doing too much when her summer expenses were paid. Martha was a person with much on her mind. Three ranch meals a day plus care of the house, garden, and Jeff kept her more than busy.

Handling Jeff and Greg were major parts of Martha's work at present, for Janet was conscious that neither had fully accepted her presence at Two Rivers. With Martha, Patty, Chuck Malone, and Sawdust she was now getting along splendidly, but to Greg and his father she was obviously something they could do without. Even though she and Greg had twice shared an experience concerning the dogs, Greg made it plain that aside from being civil, he did not care to be bothered with a girl. The matter went deeper than that: He was deeply involved with work at Two Rivers, and being asked to take Janet riding all summer was an interruption he resented even though he took her usually into the primitive territory he so enjoyed.

Time had to pass before Janet understood Jeff's antipathy, and she would not have understood then had it not been that in the small ranch house it was impossible not to overhear many things. She had fallen asleep in the porch swing one afternoon and wakened just in time to hear Jeff grumbling.

His low, hoarse voice came clearly through the door in the afternoon quiet. "But darn it, Martha! I didn't want you to have to take in boarders!"

"Now, Jeff!" Martha's voice was almost a whisper.

"We've been over that. Janet's a relative, not a boarder."

"Well, she's paying. That makes it the same. Never mind! I'll reach the place yet where I can support my family."

After that Janet took particular pains to see that he could see her hoeing in the garden, or being otherwise helpful. Jeff, however, remained distant.

Ten days after her arrival no repairs had been made on the truck, still sitting in the yard, and the sedan was still jacked up to keep it from resting on the flat tire. The thought occurred to Janet that the Kaywins would make a living easily if they didn't have to stop continually and repair things. Buildings, equipment, cars, everything on the ranch was run-down and wearing out. Obviously the Kaywins resented the situation and worried over it, but it was their problem to endure.

Then one morning Martha spoke firmly. "Greg, get that tire fixed and drive us into Jackson today. I am low on groceries."

Greg looked as aghast as though she had asked him to rob a bank. "But, Mom, we're still cutting hay. I haven't got time to fix that tire today."

"You'll have to take time, or we don't eat. I can't grow

everything in the garden, you know."

Reluctantly Greg spent an hour patching the tire, then tried to wriggle out of driving the women in. "But, Mom, you drive. Why—"

"Greg, I rarely go to town, and when I do I don't intend to spend time on the road getting myself dirt-covered fixing tires. Now get into clean clothes."

Greg would have protested further, but Jeff spoke. "Greg!"

Martha had ably recognized the probability of further tire trouble. Halfway to town a tire went flat, and Greg found the spare was equally flat. A precious half hour was spent patching an ancient inner tube before they could go on to Jackson.

Once there, Martha took her time. At the bank Janet recognized the check her father had sent ahead when Martha cashed it. She accompanied Martha as most of the check was spent carefully, sometimes almost painfully, on things the Kaywins needed. Martha invested in a new tire, bought a roll of barbed wire, several repair parts for the ranch tractor, a new axle for the truck. She looked wistfully at dress lengths displayed in a department store and bought instead a pair of stout oxfords for herself.

"Martha, Dad gave me a little money to buy something to take home with me. I'd like to buy a Western hat. Is there a place?"

There was, and for half an hour Janet tried on wide Western sombreros. Martha watched and gave advice, and Greg, sometimes amused and sometimes impatient, perched on a stool and sat out the performance.

Finally Janet found an almost-white felt with rolled brim. It fit perfectly. "I like this! Martha, what do you think?"

"I think it's exactly what you want," Martha assured her.

Janet stood in front of a mirror, tilting her head one way and another to check every angle of the hat. She turned uncertainly. "Greg, do you like it?"

Greg gave her an indulgent and thoroughly masculine grin. "Yep. Just the hat."

"Do you really think it looks all right on me?"

"Sure we think so," Greg told her. "What do you want? Chimes?"

His tone was impatiently amused, but Martha was shocked. "Greg! Your manners!"

On the spur of the moment Janet decided to abandon being patient with Greg, exchanging verbal blows with him, or enduring his patronizing manner. From now on she would reply accordingly.

"Sure," she said quickly. "Chimes. Cymbals. A brass band, too, if you've got one ready."

Behind her in the mirror she caught his surprised expression as she pretended to study the hat. A reluctant grin touched his lips as he turned away.

"I guess that will hold you," Martha told him.

Greg, at his mother's insistence, still took Janet on two weekly rides. She would have preferred going alone, but Martha seemed to feel that she could get lost too easily in the primitive country, and Janet was forced to concede that one needed a certain woods instinct to keep one's bearings in this virgin mountain land. One of these days, though, she was coming in here alone.

For the most part, the trips she and Greg made were silent. Sometimes for miles Greg seemed to forget her presence. Then, glancing back in sudden awareness, he would begin reporting on the country. One afternoon he pointed out the minute white dot that was a mountain goat perched on a crag high above them, and on the same day he showed her an eagle's nest.

Greg was following a new trail today, and half an hour

later the path descended to what appeared to be a shallow water spot. Without hesitation Greg rode Charcoal into it. Janet had long since learned that the Western horse traveled differently than any other horse. He took his time when the going was deep and difficult instead of plunging. She knew, too, that bog spots were to be found in Jackson Hole.

"How do you know what's bog and what isn't?" she had asked Chuck Malone one day.

"I dunno. You jist git so you can tell," had been his response.

Janet knew in a second that Greg had not estimated the footing correctly here. Suddenly Charcoal was flat on his side and slipping downhill, and Greg, half in and half out of the saddle, was going with him. Then Charcoal slipped over the edge of something and went completely out of sight. A shower of muddy water shot up, briefly showing Greg's face at the base of it. Then he, too, went out of sight, and all she could see was a turmoil of heaving water and mud.

With a scream Janet pulled Sawdust back and slipped from the saddle. Halfway to the brink of the marsh her own feet shot forward and she fell hard and slid. She managed to stop herself by catching a tree root, but the

mud was so slippery that she had trouble pulling herself back.

When she struggled up, she saw that Greg's head was barely showing. She started forward, but with an effort Greg blew enough mud away from his mouth to speak. "Don't! You—can't—even stand. Get your—rope."

The rope. It was a short length which Greg had fastened to her saddle to look like a riata, apparently with the idea that she would be too green to recognize the difference. With shaking hands she untied it, tossed one end out to him. Evidently he was still astride the horse, who was struggling below the surface. Greg caught the loop, managed to make a noose and slip it over his saddle horn under the mud.

Then he was coming out, hand over hand. The mud released him with a sucking sound, and his feet kept sliding backward so that he had to crawl. Janet, sitting with her feet braced against the tree root, had all she could do to hold steady.

Relieved of Greg's weight, Charcoal had risen a little, his blowing nose and erect, terrified ears showing. Greg reached solid ground; he was so mud-plastered that she hardly recognized him.

He took time only to brush a smeared forearm across his

face, making his appearance still worse. "Tie this rope to your saddle horn! Hurry! We'll have to pull Char out of there!"

Even as Janet obeyed she saw the black disappearing again. His ears went under and only his straining nose showed as he lifted it high to breathe. Mud and water churned around him.

"While I try to get hold of the reins so I can guide, bring Sawdust over in front," Greg ordered.

Greg slid far enough down the rope to reach Charcoal's head. He felt under his submerging jaw and came out with the reins. He had trouble getting back up to solid ground, but when finally he stood five feet in front of the bogged horse, he wasted no time. "Bring Sawdust over here now. Quick. There! Now take him forward, slow. Don't jerk or something will break and if it does I've lost Charcoal. Maybe . . . maybe I have anyhow!"

Janet eased Sawdust forward slowly, feeling the tension come in the rope, then run down the old cowpony's body as he began a long steady pull.

Greg was pulling up and forward on the reins. "Come on, Char. Pull. Fight it out! Come on."

Charcoal had a big stake in the struggle and he did his

best, but his very struggles seemed to carry him deeper. Had it not been for Sawdust's effort he would have disappeared for good. Finally he began inching forward and up. The mud sucked and pulled, refusing to give up its victim. Sawdust grunted and dug in his hoofs. His head dropped forward and down with effort; his back straightened, his haunches bunching like ropes.

Then they seemed to be at a standstill. Charcoal began going under again. His nostrils flared red through the mud with his frantic breathing, but he seemed to have given up the struggle.

"Come on, Char! Pull!" Greg's voice had a desperate note, as though he could not bear what he was seeing.

In response Charcoal fought forward a little. His head cleared the mass, then his back and shoulders, as if somewhere below his feet had found something solid. Then he was plunging up and out. He fell to his knees, and Greg had to leap out of the way. When the horse stood again he was weak and trembling, mud-covered and dripping, mane and tail heavy with ooze.

"Wow!" Greg exclaimed. "Imagine me getting caught in such a jam! And after all the wandering around in this country I've done!"

He sank down on an old tree trunk and let out an explosive gasp of relief. His skinny length, clothes plastered flat with mud, made Janet think of a catalpa pod, and she suddenly giggled. Greg gave her a surprised glance, then looked down at himself and began laughing, too.

"You know, if you hadn't been here and thought as quick as you did, I'd never have gotten Charcoal out of there."

"Remember the day you said 'Leave it to a girl'?" The moment the words were out Janet was aghast. How many times had she been told never to say, "I told you so"? It made people hate you. Built on past resentment of Greg, the words had popped out before she had known they were coming.

"Oh, Greg, I'm sorry! I never should have said that."

For a moment Greg said nothing, then he grinned a little shamefacedly. "Well, I guess 'Leave it to a girl' was something I shouldn't have said either. So we're even. I hand it to you. You didn't screech and run around the way most girls do. You just did what had to be done, and it saved the day for Charcoal and me."

He rose and stood looking over his beloved horse with a careful eye. Charcoal was still standing, his legs spread, dragging in air with deep gulps. "Soon as you're able, boy, we'll find that waterfall and have a bath."

Half an hour later Greg told Janet to stay back and he maneuvered Charcoal down the steep bank to the base of the waterfall and in under a thin stream of water that slanted offside. With his bandanna he washed the mud-caked horse down thoroughly, and then stood under the stream until the worst of the gooey mess was off himself.

He climbed the bank then and sat down on a rock to dry off in the sun. He gave her an odd, sidewise glance. "I suppose when you get home you'll tell all about this?"

Janet shook her head. "I think your folks have enough to worry about."

His look was grateful. "Thanks. They have."

Janet was eager to ask questions but she did not want to appear curious. Greg, she supposed, would seal up and she would never really find out much about what had caused all the Kaywin troubles.

Instead, Greg surprised her. "There's been trouble ever since we came to Jackson Hole and bought Two Rivers."

"How long have you lived here, Greg?"

"Six years. Dad and Mom had saved some money. They didn't know much about ranching but they wanted to live in this country. The main trouble is that Two Rivers isn't very large, not big enough to make enough money to buy all the things they need to run it. The second year we were here I was sick and there were hospital bills. The next year there was the same thing after Patty was born when Mom was sick. The third year Dorrity moved onto his place and we lost the prize bull Dad had paid a lot for. Then all the equipment has run down and there just isn't any money to fix it."

"What you need then is to have more money to buy more land to grow more hay, livestock, and wheat to sell so you can pay more bills?" Janet asked.

Greg scratched his head. "That about says it."

"Is that why your mother wanted to start a dude ranch?"

Greg's nod was reluctant. "Mom's always hopeful. What she couldn't seem to realize was that we were too close to the Lazy O with all their fancy dude setup to make much of an impression on dudes. Her idea was that if we could get a few this year, another year we could build cabins and stuff to accommodate a bigger crowd."

Greg was silent a moment. "There's cash in dudes all right, but I don't think it's for Two Rivers. We'd better start home."

Back at home they found Hayward, the owner of the Lazy O, standing in the yard talking to Jeff and Martha. He turned to them as they walked up. "I've just been reporting to your folks that I've lost the brown gelding with the white socks. He got out night before last, and he's probably up in the timber country somewhere, but we can't locate him."

"Is that the beautiful horse you were riding the day we met you on the trail?" Janet asked.

"He's the one, and I set a store by that horse," Hayward said emphatically. "In fact, I think so much of him that, as of now, I'm offering a hundred dollars reward to the finder."

When Hayward had gone, Janet and Greg took their horses to the stable. "I sure wish I knew where that gelding was," Greg muttered half to himself. "A hundred dollars . . . gee!"

It seemed to Janet that of the whole Two Rivers outfit Chuck Malone was the only one who did not have problems, whose mood was perpetually sunny. By now he teased her unmercifully, and often with a dead-pan expression which she had not yet learned to single out from seriousness.

At the supper table that night he gave her a level look.

"See any snakes around here, Janet?"

She had never thought of snakes, but it seemed reasonable that they would be present in a country containing marshes. "No, I haven't, not yet. Should I be on the watch for them?"

Chuck shrugged elaborately. "Not any more. There aren't any snakes in the Hole now. Or maybe there's one if he's still livin'."

"Now? You mean there were once?"

"Oh, yeah. Everybody around here knew that we'd managed to get rid of all the rattlers but one, a big old boy who had fooled us all and hid out. One night I was camped out up in the primitive and I woke up and felt somethin' heavy on my chest. There he was with his head lifted. I could see him movin' up and down when I breathed in an' out. Imagine my feelin's—one snake left in all of Jackson Hole and he had to spend the night right on my chest!"

Chuck let out an explosive breath and shook his head. "I sure was worried!"

The supper table was very silent. Greg ate with his head down. Martha's lips twitched, but she steadied them and listened quietly.

"But, Chuck! What on earth did you do?" Janet pleaded, as Chuck did not continue.

"Do!" Chuck exclaimed. "There was nothin' I could do. I just shut my eyes and went back to sleep."

7   *Mr. Hayward's Horse*

For the next week, it seemed to Janet that every time she turned a corner Greg asked if she had seen Hayward's gelding.

"Do you think he's hiding under a rock, or something?" she asked one day.

Greg grinned a little ruefully. "No, but I've got a feeling he's not too far away. Maybe, though, that's just because I could use a hundred dollars."

On Saturday afternoon of that same week Martha drove Jeff into town to see if the doctor would permit his discarding his crutches. Patty had elected to go with her mother. Chuck and Greg were at work finishing up the hay job so that they would be ready to start harvesting wheat within the next ten days. From where she sat on the porch with a new book her mother had sent the day before, Janet could see the whole forty acres of waving green heads just beginning to turn gold.

Only that morning Jeff had looked out the kitchen window at it. "Best we've ever grown. Sure hope nothing happens to it."

It was the only voluntary remark he had made to Janet in the weeks she had been at Two Rivers.

The day was drowsy-warm. Machinery sounded distantly from the hay field. In the corral Sawdust neighed suddenly, and Janet felt the urge to ride. She was saddling when the thought came that this was an ideal time to take an experimental trip into primitive territory. With rising enthusiasm for the idea, she returned to the house for her bathing suit. Perhaps she could wade along the edges of one of the lakes she had seen.

She took the short trail up to Pacific Creek, and as she loped past the Dorrity acreage she saw the old man out in the pasture with a visitor. Dorrity's companion was a short, broadly built man who strode about the meadow with his head down watching an instrument he held before him. Janet could not see what he carried, but both men seemed deeply intent on observing it. Neither so much as glanced up as she passed.

With a feeling of excitement Janet entered primitive territory on the trail over which Greg had first taken her. This trip was all the more fascinating because she was taking it alone. She planned to go only a short distance to keep from getting lost.

Half an hour later she glimpsed through the trees the tiny jewel-like lake where she and Greg had listened to the drake singing to the hen. Now, pausing to listen, Janet heard a new sound. Soft quacking was broken by faint baby gabblings.

Moving as quietly as possible, Janet found a place off the trail where she could tie Sawdust, then crawled through bushes until she could look down on the duck parents and eight ducklings floating on the surface of the lake. The small ones followed their mother like magnets, drifting where she drifted, closing in around her when she quacked warningly.

Janet giggled to herself as the drake suddenly upended, his short tail briefly erect, and went completely under. As though he had signaled, all his eight children followed suit, each leaving a brief rippling circle on the surface. The mother swam about their group vanishing point calmly until one at a time they surfaced like corks.

Janet moved quietly out of the bushes and sat on the bank. The ducks swam to the opposite side, wary but not alarmed, and she continued to sit until finally they paid her almost no attention. Then in the shelter of the bushes she donned her bathing suit and waded into the lake. The ducks moved away, and she swam after them, making as little commotion as possible. The family seemed to wait until she reached a certain point, then after a warning quack from father, all ten turned their tails skyward and disappeared.

Treading water, Janet waited until they came up off to her right, and then swam toward them again. Again the ducks vanished. The situation became a game with the duck family definitely having the upper hand.

Abruptly the game broke. The drake had just come up and shaken the water from his head when he gave a note of warning, sharper, harsher than before. The family turned tail and swam directly across the lake, climbed out on the bank and disappeared in the undergrowth.

Then Janet heard a sound. Boots were coming up the trail, hitting bluntly and rapidly. She swam hastily back to

her entrance point and in the bushes scrambled into shirt and jeans.

She was not a moment too soon. Old Man Dorrity appeared on the trail, a sack over his shoulder. Halfway around the lake he paused when he saw the ripples of water still widening out from the point where Janet had emerged. He frowned, staring about, and Janet huddled in fright, hoping that Sawdust made no sound.

Finally, as though convinced some animal had made the ripples, Dorrity went on, but not before Janet noticed that there was a small hole in the sack he carried, and from it grains spilled onto the trail.

She breathed a deep sigh of relief when he had disappeared from sight, and she waited at least fifteen minutes before she went out to bend over the evidence scattered on the trail.

"Oats!" she whispered. "Horses and chickens—they eat oats. He hasn't a horse and he wouldn't have his chickens up here."

The thought that popped into her mind was so astonishing that she felt her mouth opening and closing in reaction. Then she was off down the trail after Dorrity, peering around every bend to be sure she did not come upon him unexpectedly. She was too afraid of the recluse to want to be seen.

For half a mile Dorrity's tracks were distinct, then she had to retrace her steps to the point where a trail of oats showed that he had left the path and cut off into the timber.

Trying to make use of the woodsman's instinct that seemed so natural to Greg, Janet took note of trees, rocks, and bushes as she cautiously followed the oats. Obviously this was not Dorrity's first trip. Grain previously trampled down into the grass, the trail of crushed leaves and grass, these told her Dorrity had passed this way often of late. Then, as she was peering from behind a boulder, she heard a horse nicker, the sound less than a hundred yards ahead.

Dorrity was not in sight and Janet sprinted for a ledge ahead and to the left. She scrambled up the side and dropped panting to look perhaps fifty feet beyond it to where Dorrity was pouring oats into a wooden box. A handsome gelding was plunging his nose hungrily into the contents.

The sight was exactly what she had expected to see, but now she squinted her eyes and stared at the horse. *Was* this Hayward's gelding? That animal had had four white socks and a star; this horse had no white at all. Janet blinked and rubbed her eyes. This horse certainly had the same proud carriage, the restiveness of the other. Dorrity put out a hand toward the animal, which dodged away, upsetting the box of grain. The hermit yelled angrily, then glanced over his shoulder as though fearful of being heard.

He tossed the box aside so the horse could eat off the ground, then went about testing the poles and stakes he had set up and strung with wire to make a fence. The ledge on which Janet lay was a semicircle of rock probably fifteen feet high, and by fastening the wire from one end to the other, Dorrity had created an ideal corral, one that even had a tiny spring trickling along an inner wall. If a person wanted to hide a horse, he could not have found a better location.

When Dorrity had gone, Janet slipped down off the ledge and went close. The horse, haltered and dragging a long rope so that he could be easily caught if necessary in the small enclosure, snorted and moved away as she approached, but she was close enough to see that his hair just above the hoofs was darker than that above. She knew horses often did darken at that point, but it seemed to her that a certain irregularity, a slightly different shade of brown betrayed an artificial job. She moved to where she could better study the gelding's star, and found that a darker brown showed there, too, a color that did not seem quite natural.

"You've been painted," Janet told him. There was no doubt that this was Hayward's horse. "Now I wonder if I should take you home or go for help."

The gelding settled the question. Without warning he reared and squealed, shaking his head and flattening his ears. He had been locked behind high wire and rock in this sixty-foot corral until he was restless and angry.

"You'd be too much for me," Janet decided.

When she reached Sawdust she hoped that Dorrity, on his return trip, had not sighted the palomino, and as she rode on the return trail, she watched around every bend to avoid catching up with him. When she had crossed Pacific Creek, she cut off through the timber to avoid his house and went directly out into the hay field where Greg and Chuck were working.

"I've found Mr. Hayward's horse," she announced with calm she was far from feeling.

Their astonished expressions were all she could have desired. The two men did not even wait to leave a note for Jeff and Martha. With Greg on Charcoal and Chuck riding behind Janet, they had reached the scene in the timber just as the sun was losing itself behind the Tetons. The anxious gelding was belling even before they stopped beside the fence.

"So help me!" Chuck exclaimed. "She's right! That horse's been dyed."

"I bet the critter has been penned in that two-by-four space ever since Hayward lost him," Greg said. "He looks as though he's ready to jump out of his skin. How are we going to manage getting him home?"

"Maybe you better ride him." Chuck suggested the idea with a grin, but Greg took him seriously.

"All right. Let's catch and saddle him. You can ride Charcoal home bareback, and Janet can probably handle Sawdust with this nag's halter."

Chuck was immediately alarmed. "Listen, boy! It's all Hayward can do to handle that critter sometimes. You'd better not try it!"

Greg was already pulling up a fence stake. "Help me catch and hold him."

Catching the horse was no problem with the dragging rope, but he snorted and dodged as Greg walked hand over hand up the rope. When finally he stood at the horse's head, he took his time soothing the animal, rubbing his fingers under the headstall, blowing softly against his nose, talking to him quietly. "Bring the saddle," he told Chuck finally.

Reluctantly Chuck brought Charcoal's saddle. The gelding stamped, pawed, and kicked at Greg when he tightened the cinch. "Now trade this halter for Janet's bridle."

"Kid, I still think—" Chuck began.

"Now, tear the fence down and everybody get out of the way when I go up," Greg told them.

"Oh, Greg! Be careful!" Janet begged.

Chuck held the gelding's bridle as Greg went up, but the horse reared, tossing him aside, and plunged out of the corral in a series of buck-jumps designed to get his head down. Greg did not make the mistake of trying to do rodeo riding. He hung to the saddle horn and hauled up and back on the reins so the horse could not get his head down and buck him off. For half a mile he let the fiery creature take his own speed. Then when he reached the main trail he hauled him up and turned back to meet Janet and Chuck. The gelding was still full of mettle, but he was manageable now. Chuck and Janet hurried to keep the pace behind him.

"Greg, are you going to pass right along Dorrity's place?"

He thought about her question a moment. "No, even

though it'll be full dark by then, I think we'll cut off at Cottonwood Flat and reach the highway. It's about three miles farther, but maybe it'll keep us out of trouble. If he saw us it would be one more thing to blame the Kaywins for."

At the Lazy O an hour later music and the ring of laughter sounded from the house; Janet had to pound on the door to make anyone hear.

"We found your horse," she told Hayward when he finally came. She had never felt so proud.

In a second all the beautiful racket had shut off, and Hayward's summer guests poured out into the barnyard where Hayward had already turned on the pole light.

"But that isn't . . ." Hayward began. He walked all the way around the horse, his mouth hanging ludicrously open. "But it is!" he exclaimed. "Piper, boy, where you been?" The beautiful animal had reached toward his master to be petted.

Hayward turned to Greg. "Where—?"

Greg gestured toward Janet. "She found him. Let her tell it."

"But Greg rode him in. I never could have gotten him out." When she had finished her story, Hayward stood

shaking his head in bafflement.

"That old hermit! Who'd ever believe he'd find a horse and paint him!"

"Do you think he stole the horse out of your corral?"

Hayward shook his head at Greg's question. "No, the horse got out through a break in the fence. My man saw him go. Dorrity probably caught him with that dragging rope and had an idea for getting him away and selling him. He didn't have it figured out yet how he'd do all that, and you, Janet, ran into him before he got it accomplished. Well, you folks come in while I write out a check. It's worth every cent of what I promised."

While they waited, Greg called home to tell his mother what had become of the three of them. He hung up grinning. "Mom was about to call the sheriff."

Meanwhile Janet had been looking around the spacious and luxurious Lazy O ranch house. As Greg had said, there was money in dudes. She knew Hayward's acreage was only slightly larger than Two Rivers, and Janet estimated there must be at least thirty paying guests present. No wonder Martha had felt that if the Kaywins could get started "duding," their problems would be solved. Outside there had been the big barnyard and the big sturdy barn.

Behind the house she had been able to see, by the glow of the pole light, the rows of small guest cabins. Now inside she was sitting in a large lounge living room with deep windows on the front and on the inner wall a great fireplace. Deep chairs and tables with magazines were grouped, the whole designed for comfort, for leisure, and for people who could pay the price.

Hayward had come back into the room. He sat at a desk, waving his checkbook. "Who gets this reward?"

"Janet," Greg said promptly.

"Greg!" she retorted.

Hayward sat grinning while several watching guests chuckled over the ensuing argument.

"I know," Janet told Hayward. "Make the check out to Greg's mother. That's what I'd do with it anyhow, and I think Greg would prefer it."

The matter was settled thus. Greg, who would have refused the check for himself, could hardly refuse for his mother.

"Will you do anything to Mr. Dorrity?" Janet asked when Hayward, with a flourish, had given her the check.

The dude rancher leaned back in his swivel desk chair until it screamed a protest. "Fifteen minutes ago I'd have said I'd prosecute him. We certainly have the goods on him. On the other hand our chief witnesses live next door to him, and they've already had trouble enough. Janet, do you think he saw you?"

Janet shook her head. "Not me, but he could have seen Sawdust where I had him tied. I just don't know."

Hayward considered. "If he did he could have put two and two together and come up with the fact that the Kaywins were spoiling his plans again. No, I don't think I'll prosecute. I have my horse back."

The rancher rose. "You folks better get on home before your folks worry themselves to death about you. We're having a square dance here a week from tonight, and we're going to have guests of honor—the whole Kaywin family! Now don't forget. If you don't come we're coming after you."

At home Martha was sputtering like a setting hen who had been driven off her eggs. "The way you kids run foul of that man amazes me! Can't you find any place to go except where he is?"

"Nope," Greg told her placidly. "He comes where we are. Janet's got something for you, Mom."

They made formal presentation of the check, and

Martha, pleased, flustered, protesting and excited, tried to make Janet keep it.

Janet put determined hands behind her back. "I can't cash it. It's not even made out to me. If you don't cash and use it, it'll never be cashed and nobody will get any good out of it."

Martha protested further and found her family adamant. There were tears in her eyes when she finally yielded and thrust the check inside her purse.

Janet ate a late supper with the others and went immediately to bed. It seemed a long time since she had decided to ride into primitive territory alone.

"I wonder," she thought just before she fell asleep, "if Mr. Dorrity did see Sawdust on his way out."

8   *"Storybook Stuff!"*

For a few days life at Two Rivers was quiet and everyone was glad of it. Martha was occupied with canning her garden produce. Jeff, released from his crutches, made a slow tour of the yard and corrals several times a day; he was more cheerful now that he could walk again, and occasionally he gave Janet his slow, thoughtful smile. She had been asked to repeat the story of finding Piper several times for his special benefit.

On her next ride toward Pacific Creek she saw that Dorrity and the short man with the instrument were again walking about the pasture. She rode quietly by, wondering if Dorrity had found any reason yet to think she was connected with the disappearance of Hayward's gelding from his improvised corral in the timber.

She rode only a short distance into primitive country that day, for she had started late in the day. As she crossed Cottonwood Flat and rode down the bank of Pacific Creek on the return trip, her thoughts were on the coming dance at the Lazy O. All week her anticipation had been increasing.

Lifting her boots high against the saddle skirts, Janet watched the water swirl around Sawdust's legs as he picked his careful way among the rocks. Then suddenly he "spooked." Squatting, he wheeled in midstream, slipped on a rock, and went down into the water with a terrific lurch that flung Janet out of the saddle and away from him.

Water swirled over her head, and she felt herself being carried downstream. She was upside down, and her head scraped along the bottom until she managed to push down with her hands and shove herself upward. She was promptly knocked off her feet again by the current, but as she was carried along she saw willow branches bending over the water. She caught them and gripped hard, feeling the slender wet boughs slipping through her grasp, but she shoved her water-filled boots down and pushed until she got leverage enough to hold herself in place.

Choking and gasping, she managed to drag in a great gulp of air, and after a few deep breaths she crawled shakily out on the bank and looked upstream to where Sawdust stood on the Cottonwood Flat side, looking back over his shoulder at the opposite bank. Her glance followed the pitch of his ears and there, half hidden by the bushes, at the very point where his land joined the path down to Pacific Creek, stood Old Man Dorrity. Either his presence had frightened Sawdust or he had deliberately done something to startle the palomino. Whichever it was, the hermit found the situation hilarious. Holding his sides, he rocked back and forth with laughter. Janet found herself shaking with something besides a scraped head, weakness, and cold water. There was a fiendish quality to his mirth, a delight at having caused trouble.

Appalled, Janet could only watch for a moment. Then she was more angry than she had ever been in her life. "What are you doing over there?" she yelled above the roar of the water.

Dorrity reached into the bushes behind him and drew out a long strand of barbed wire already fastened to the end post at the trail. Deliberately he crossed the path which

Greg had once told her really belonged to Dorrity but which he had finally left open for those who needed to cross Pacific Creek.

"Young lady, I am fencin' off my propity." He gave a shrill, joyous cackle. "This leetle strip ain't open to the public no more." He pulled the wire tight and wrapped it around a tree trunk that stood at the edge of the water, then turned and pointed a grimy finger at her. "An' if I find you or anybody else interferin' in my affairs, I'll call the sheriff, I will!"

Janet had her breath back now. As she pulled her wet self up onto an equally wet horse, she was thinking that Dorrity was practically declaring that she was the one who had interfered in the case of Hayward's gelding. He was warning her.

She pulled Sawdust around to face him. "Good! I'll be glad to see the sheriff. I have plenty of witnesses that you deal in other people's property sometimes, and probably the sheriff would like to know that."

The blaze of sheer hate from Dorrity seemed to leap Pacific Creek. Janet knew immediately that she had said something better left omitted, and the Kaywins were just as much involved as though they had been the ones who had said it. Wheeling Sawdust, she kicked him hard in the ribs and galloped down the bank of Pacific Creek to connect with the highway and reach home.

Her hair and clothing had dried by the time she turned off the highway into the narrow country lane, and she decided to say nothing about her adventure to the family. They could do nothing and there was no use in worrying them.

Just as she turned off the highway she found a station wagon parked beside the road. A man was getting a can out of the back and he raised a hand as she started to pass.

"Howdy, young lady. I've run out of gas. Would you know anybody who has gas at their place?"

"The Kaywins, down this lane, have a storage tank. They'll probably help you out."

She loped on ahead to tell Jeff, her mind meanwhile trying to figure out where she had seen this man before.

Jeff was waiting at the tank by the time the visitor arrived. The man sank down on the well-curbing while Jeff filled his can. "You know this old chap up the road?" he asked. "The one who owns the pasture just before you reach Pacific Creek?"

Janet recognized him then. This was the man she had

seen in the pasture with Dorrity on two occasions.

"We know him," Jeff replied dryly. Neither he nor Martha, standing near, volunteered any further information, and the silence extended.

Then the short bulky man burst forth. "What kind of a nut is that old boy? I worked that pasture of his over for a whole day. Couldn't find a thing. After I left he called me back and made me do it again. Know what? When I still couldn't locate a million for him he got sore. Told me I didn't know what I was doin'! Me, Sam Burnett!"

Martha's expression was amazed. "A million? What on earth did he want you to find?"

The evening was cooling rapidly, but Sam Burnett sank back against the pump and mopped perspiration from a sun-reddened face and balding head with his bandanna. "I earn a living doing Geiger counter work for anybody that wants it. For a hobby, I hunt buried loot. Started in my teens. Know all the old maps and half the locations in the States where supposedly stuff has been buried."

Burnett's face became increasingly indignant as he told his story. "Him telling me! Somewhere he heard I'd said there was a cache buried in Jackson Hole, and he wrote asking me to come and counter his land. So I've taken a whole day on two occasions to go over that pasture of his, yard for yard. The counter never showed a thing either time, and he accused me of not trying. I told him if I did it again it would be another fee, and only an hour ago he ordered me off his property. Told me he'd shoot me if he ever saw me around again! Whew, the old coot's crazy! Never offered me a bite to eat today, either."

He looked so frustrated that Martha could not forebear offering an invitation. "Stop and eat with us, Mr. Burnett. You look exhausted."

Burnett protested, but he was easily persuaded. He had put in a hard day. Fed and refreshed, he turned into an interesting conversationalist. He recounted tales of the places he had worked, the success and failure of various mining expeditions, but the Kaywins found him at his best when he told of his various hunts for buried treasure.

"But is there really very much buried treasure in this country?" Janet asked him. "And what is this story about loot in Jackson Hole?"

As she asked the question Janet was conscious that Martha leaned forward over the table to hear Burnett's answer. She seemed almost to hold her breath.

Burnett smiled as he answered. "That's hard to answer

with one word. There's treasure in a lot of cases, but often it's buried so deep or the directions deliberately tangled to confuse a hunter. Often, too, the loot's already been removed but nobody knows that. This Jackson Hole situation is something I've always wanted to investigate, and I suppose that's why I was so enthusiastic when Dorrity wrote me. Supposedly, Spaniards came this far north and left it. There are no real directions and no map. A man would just have to scan the whole territory with a Geiger counter, which is almost impossible."

Martha sat back, her breath coming out in a faint sigh. "It sounds just like an adventure yarn."

Burnett glanced around the table at the faces of his hosts. "All treasure stories sound that way. You don't believe me, do you?"

Janet followed his glance. Jeff appeared skeptical and so did Chuck. Greg obviously was trying to keep rational and calm about the whole story, but Martha, her eyes wide, was drinking in every word. She hardly seemed to breathe. On several occasions Janet had felt sorry for Martha, but never more than now.

"Well," Jeff replied to Burnett, "it does sound a little—"

"But it's not farfetched!" Burnett was vehement. "I'd

wager my bottom dollar that somewhere in this Jackson Hole country there's a cache of stuff. There may be argument about who hid it and what it is, but I'll bet it's still here."

For a moment there was silence. Patty finally broke it in her slow-spoken fashion. "Then why don't you go dig it up?"

The slightly embarrassing interval broke on laughter, and as it subsided Burnett answered her. "All right, young lady, I'll tell you what I'll do. I'll go get my car and my Geiger counter and I'll go over *your* pasture just to pay for this excellent supper."

A man of action, Burnett rose from the table and was out of the house and down the road within a few minutes. He returned to park his station wagon alongside the ripening wheat next to the pasture, and within another few minutes he was moving out across the pasture with Chuck at his side.

Jeff settled into his chair on the porch to watch, an expression of tolerant amusement on his dour face. Martha sat on the step. She was stiffly upright, her absorbed gaze following Burnett's every motion.

"She wants to believe he'll find something more than

anything in the world," Janet told herself. She had not been blind lately. The wheat harvest was close, but so was the payment on the mortgage and the interest. There was a question whether there would be money enough from the crop to pay it, and there was also the worry concerning what could happen to the wheat in that week's interval. Storms, wet weather, stock breaking through the rickety old fences to trample the heavy heads into the earth, any or all of these could happen within that week. That fact alone explained why one or the other of the parent Kaywins seemed to be always looking out the kitchen window at that wheat field.

Martha twisted on the step. "Jeff . . .?"

"Now, Martha," Jeff told her, "don't start hoping. We left fairy tales behind years ago. A stranger with a Geiger counter arrives and searches the Kaywin pasture for treasure. He finds it and we live happily and wealthily ever after! No, I think we Kaywins will still rely on wheat and live-stock, in small amounts and for small profits. Anyway, we eat."

Greg, sitting beside his mother, turned to give his father a look of unspoken protest. Janet sensed that he wanted desperately to believe with his mother but felt his father was right. After a few moments he rose and went down to the pasture.

Dusk had fallen, but the men in the pasture kept moving about. Now and then a match flared as they examined the instrument. Burnett was along the fence that divided the wheat from the meadow and was moving toward the house. Suddenly he stopped. Then he backed up a few steps, only to move forward again. Voices in low discussion carried faintly on the night air. Janet could almost feel Martha straining to hear what was said.

Through the dimness they saw the three men crawl through the fence into the wheat field and start moving about. Jeff leaned forward and spoke irritably. "Now they're starting to tramp down the crop! I never should have let—"

"Oh, Jeff!" Martha cried out sharply. "Just this once, let it go!"

Jeff subsided, but he kept moving irritably in his chair and muttering. Now the men were moving out into the wheat field, only a few yards and then retreating to the fence line. Once they went back into the pasture. Martha hardly seemed to breathe.

Half an hour passed and then the three men came directly

to the house with Burnett striding purposefully in the lead. "Mr. Kaywin, I've found sign! There's something underground right at your fence line."

Jeff was not about to be convinced so easily. "Some old iron a rancher dropped off there maybe?" he inquired dryly. "This is one of the oldest spreads in Jackson Hole, you know."

"But Dad, I saw the Geiger counter myself! It registered."

Burnett must have dealt with disbelief before, Janet thought. He answered quietly. "You could be quite right, Mr. Kaywin. It could be old metal. A Geiger counter doesn't lie, however, and how are you going to know what you've got until you dig for it? Wouldn't you prefer to know whether it's merely an old harrow buried there, or whether, maybe in this one chance in a million, you've got something you'd hate to miss?"

Jeff's reply came without a pause. "Certainly I'd like to know, but another thing is even more certain: I haven't the cash to pay you for your time to find the answer."

An awkward pause developed. Burnett slapped his bald spot sharply. "Let's go inside and get away from these mosquitoes."

Martha and Greg went immediately inside with Burnett following. Jeff limped in reluctantly and he remained standing while everyone else pulled chairs up to the dining table. They sat looking at him steadily until finally, in embarrassment, he sat down with them.

"Mr. Kaywin, I'm sufficiently interested in what my Geiger counter says about that spot to make a deal with you. If you'll look up such matters you'll find that it's a customary deal, and I will put it in writing to assure your rights. The digger furnishes the machinery and pays all expenses. If nothing is found, the owner of the property is out nothing, but if something is uncovered, the two share half and half. Could anything be more fair than that?"

"You mean, Mr. Burnett, that it costs us absolutely nothing for you to find what that is down there?" Martha's voice was tense.

"That's exactly it, Mrs. Kaywin. Perhaps you think I seem urgent, and I am. The situation is this: Beginning two weeks from today I'm due at Rawlins for an excavation job. My bulldozer outfit is over at Du Noir, where I just finished a job for a man, and I probably won't have that heavy machinery this close again for years. I've always wanted to do this hunt in Jackson Hole, and I can't think of a more fortunate combination of circumstances. I could be digging, you know, by day after tomorrow."

Jeff sat stubbornly. "But what if you do find something? What would it be? Bullion? Coins?"

"It could be either, and it could be ornaments of some value. I won't hide one fact. Sometimes we find things that have no value at all. That's my hard luck, mostly. On the other hand, a man in this business has to remember that occasionally it takes a little time to learn the value of what is found. If you don't know the ropes, you're likely to sell coins to the Government just at gold or silver value, whereas a museum would pay much more. For instance, I found a doubloon once for which the Government would have paid me thirty dollars an ounce just as gold. I got five hundred dollars for it from a coin collector. If we find anything at all, it will be that sort of investigation that will make the money for us."

It took another hour of argument before Jeff finally gave in. Burnett rose immediately. "I'll bring my bulldozer and your contract here by tomorrow night."

When he had gone Martha let out a tired sigh. "Wouldn't it be wonderful if he really found something!"

"Sure would!" Greg said. "And we're not out a thing!"

Jeff rose stiffly and turned toward the bedroom, as he looked his family over wryly. "Now listen, all of you! When this guy has come and gone, leaving us with a hole in the ground, don't say I didn't warn you. Buried treasure went out with Laffite at New Orleans."

His remarks did not in the least dampen Kaywin hopes. "And I thought we'd have to sell the place to pay the mortgage!" Martha exclaimed.

Greg's face had been shining with anticipation, but now as he watched his mother, his expression sobered. "Mom, I sure hope you're right, but, as Dad says, don't start paying that mortgage with buried treasure. Not yet!"

Burnett was as good as his word. By the following night he had arrived with his bulldozer and his contract. "Where shall I put it nights? It's brand-new."

Jeff's reply was faintly amused. "I think it will fit in the entry to the old hay barn over there. That'll keep the dew off the paint. Have Greg back out the sedan."

Together Burnett and Greg moved the fence line farther out into the pasture so that the wheat would be left as undisturbed as possible. By the end of the first day he had scraped a place perhaps fifty feet in diameter in the pasture and was preparing to deepen the area the next day.

"We have to work pretty slowly," he explained to Greg whom he had shown how to start and stop the machine. "Dig down too sharply and we might not leave enough to be of value to anybody."

Burnett was staying with the Kaywins during the operation, and he was at work by daylight and he did not cease until dark. "I'll say one thing," Jeff admitted grudgingly, "if he's fooling us he's sure doing it on his own time."

Hayward rode into the yard on the evening of the second day's digging. He pulled his prancing Piper, whose star and four white socks had been bleached out to their original color, to a halt and stared at the bald spot in the pasture. "What on earth?"

Jeff grinned at him. "Didn't know we went in for storybook stuff, did you? We're digging for treasure, a great big pile of it left by the Spaniards three centuries ago."

"In Jackson Hole?" Hayward's tone was squeaky with surprise.

"Honest," Jeff assured him blandly. "Never heard the yarn before, did you?"

Hayward's brow furrowed as he thought. "Well, yes. There has been a yarn like that told among the older people in Jackson Hole, but it had been mostly forgotten with the decades. I haven't heard it since I was a kid. Well, what do you know!"

After a few moments of watching with his mouth slightly open, Hayward turned again to Jeff. "Just came down to remind you the dance is tomorrow night, and that the Kaywins are still our guests of honor. We want all of you, Chuck, too, and bring your treasure digger. Our guests sure will be surprised. I've issued a blanket invitation to the whole community."

"We'll try to bring them all," Martha assured him.

9   *Too Many Questions*

When the Kaywin group walked into the Lazy O lounge on the following evening, the dance was already in full swing. Four dance sets were inside and two more on the terrace outside.

"Hey, look who's comin'!" The caller standing before the great stone fireplace with his microphone broke his call in the middle and hailed the guests of honor. Cheers shook the beams as the guests responded.

"We got a couple people here maybe most of you folks haven't met. That cute little number with the bangs is Janet Lennon and most of you have seen her on television—youngest of the singin' Lennon sisters—in case you haven't met her. That sawed-off guy is Sam Burnett, prospectin' for gold, so we hear, over on the Kaywin ranch. We always knew there was gold in the Kaywin family. They're it! What we didn't know was that they had it in the pasture, too. Break your sets, folks, and pull in the guests of honor. Let's dance!"

Greg and Janet found a spot in the nearest set, and Chuck and Martha were absorbed into another amid the gasps of surprise and the cheers from the assembled crowd. Jeff and Burnett found chairs on the side lines to watch. Martha had had some difficulty persuading the two men to come, Burnett for fear he would not waken early enough the next morning to get in a day's work and Jeff because he did not like leaving the ranch unattended. They had been coaxed into coming because only a half mile of distance separated the two ranches on the country road that led off the main highway.

For the next hour it seemed to Janet that she was literally spinning. These ranch folk took their dancing with enthusiasm. Voices shouted with laughter, feet shuffled. Age did not matter. To the Kaywin's surprise, Burnett later strode across the floor and asked Mrs. Ames, an elderly woman from a ranch home, to dance. He bowed with a flourish and she came to her feet and was ready to go before he had time to straighten, and she led him through the calls expertly.

Youngsters were everywhere. Janet especially noticed a freckled crew of seven, as much alike as lima beans except for size, who continually surrounded the refreshment area. Hayward had dragged in a huge black iron soap kettle of ancient vintage and filled it with cracked ice. Soft-drink bottles sprouted from the ice in every direction, and guests were to help themselves. The freckled crew took the invitation at face value, and bottle after bottle vanished as the dance progressed. Hayward was kept busy refilling the kettle.

"Who are those kids?" Janet asked him during an intermission as she helped him shove more bottles down into the ice.

"Wisnosky kids who live in that shack down on the corner where the road joins the highway," he told her. "Let 'em have their fun. I only do this once a year. That crew fights for all they get, and it doesn't come easy. It's only pop."

Janet danced the next set with Chuck and then went outside to cool off as a new set started. She slipped around the corner of the house and stood in the darkness drinking in the beauty of the night, the stars that seemed to hang low and brilliant, the breeze, cooler now and coming in from the east. As her eyes became accustomed to the darkness, she drew a deep, happy breath.

Behind a lilac bush across the yard something moved, something larger than a dog, smaller than a horse. She stared through the gloom as it moved from bush to bush, cautious and skulking in its hunched bulk. A little frightened, Janet flattened herself against the side of the house and watched.

The shape had reached and passed all the bushes and waited an interval behind the last. She could make out now that it was a man, his head moving from side to side as he peered toward a window of the lounge. There was something familiar about that shape.

The man moved furtively from behind his protecting screen and up beside the light flung out the window from the lounge.

With a gasp Janet recognized Dorrity. Standing just outside the light, he bent one way and another, peering inside for several minutes. Then as quietly as he had come he vanished into the shrubbery.

"Buffalo Gals" had just ended as she re-entered the

lounge and hunted up Hayward. "Did you invite Mr. Dorrity?"

The rancher gave her a puzzled glance. "Why, not specifically. I just gave a blanket invitation to everybody around. If he'd come I wouldn't have thrown him out, but naturally I hardly expected him. Why?"

"I was just outside cooling off, and I saw him slip up and look in the window."

"Dorrity?"

He thought about the matter after she nodded, then dismissed it. "Maybe the old boy wanted to come in and didn't have the nerve, so he just peeked. Come on, Janet, there goes the music for a polka."

It was the middle of the evening and round-dance time. After the polka with Hayward, she danced the "Rye Waltz" with the caller, and then the "Varsoviana" with Hayward. As it finished he drew her up to the mike.

"Folks, this evening would never be complete unless we heard from this young lady. Janet, how about some songs?"

This was vacation time and Janet would gladly have avoided entertaining, but with cheers already rising, she could hardly refuse Hayward's request. After a brief conference with the fiddler on what they could do together, she sang "Billy Boy," noticing, as she sang the tender phrases of the old song, the reminiscent smiles on the faces of older folks. "Home on the Range" brought smiles from young and old alike and noisy urging for an encore.

She decided on a fast-paced song to get people in the humor for dancing again. "Come on!" she cried. " 'Yellow Rose of Texas.' Everybody sing with me."

They sang with gusto, almost drowning her out by the end of the first chorus. As she watched her crowd and sang, Janet's glance crossed the east window and stopped. In her astonishment she stopped singing and stared. Nothing but space lay between Lazy O and Two Rivers, a half mile of it unbroken by hills or trees. Near the Kaywin place a faint glow lay along the ground. Then a tongue of flame showed.

Heads wheeled, chairs scraped as she pointed wordlessly out the window. The song died. "Fire!" yelled Chuck. "Fire at the ranch!"

Dancers crowded out the door. Feet pounded, car motors raced, and dust rose. Janet managed to crowd into the sedan with Chuck, Greg, and Burnett, and they were in the lead as they raced down the road.

"It's a grass fire down in the pasture!" Greg exclaimed when they were close enough to see. "And the wind's in the east! It could take the buildings."

"My bulldozer!" Burnett cried in anguish. "Hurry, Greg!"

Greg almost turned the car over wheeling into the yard. Everybody was out in a second, and Chuck and Greg made for the barn and returned with an armload of seed sacks which they plunged into the horse trough. By now the yard was full of men who grabbed wet sacks and rushed out to flay the edges of the crawling grass fire with them. The blaze was coming directly toward the old hay barn that housed the bulldozer. Unless stopped, it would also take the barn and corrals that lay beyond it.

Burnett had the motor of the bulldozer going now and he came backing out of the hay-barn entry. He wheeled the machine around. "Out of the way, everybody!"

Even as he bawled the order, flames drove the men back and seemed almost to leap at the dry old buildings. A few bales and some loose hay lay on the near side and they went up like tinder. Disregarding the building, Burnett lowered the blade of his machine and cut a six-foot swath off the face of the earth between hay barn and pasture. He went the length of the line of blazing grass, turned about and came back to encircle the hay barn completely and cut the fire away from the barn and corral unless sparks bridged the gap.

Jeff had arrived and he swung toward the stable with a long hitching step. "Throw wet sacks up on the roof!" he shouted at the men who had backed out of the path of the bulldozer.

Dipping their sacks again in the horse trough, they tossed them up to Greg and Chuck who laid soaking lengths on the roof side that faced the fire. Sparks, carried by the east wind, were falling everywhere. They caught bits of hay in the corral and men stamped them out. The roof began to steam, but the flames were dying now, covered with loose dirt, beaten out by boots, smothered with soaked sacks. Finally the Kaywins and Hayward's smoke-blackened guests stood about watching the charred pasture which the headlights of cars showed still smoking faintly here and there. An odd silence fell.

Janet sought out Greg. "Who could have started that fire?"

"I'll guess once," he retorted. "Burnett didn't find anything on Dorrity's place, but he's digging on ours. That old hermit would do anything to keep us from benefiting."

"I suppose so. He hates me especially."

Greg stared at her from red-rimmed eyes. "Why you in particular?"

They moved away from the others while she filled him in on the details of her watery meeting with the hermit at Pacific Creek. She shuddered at the memory of his boisterous joy at her predicament. Greg was almost speechless with anger, but before he could express himself adequately, talk broke out among the men behind them.

"Jeff, you must have a million under that fence line, or nobody'd be burning you out like this!" Hayward's booming voice was jocular, but his tone sobered as he added, "What on earth could have started that fire anyhow?"

Janet and Greg had moved back among the crowd, and Hayward's glance, looking balefully about as though to find the culprit, crossed her own. He paused, eyebrows lifting in startled recollection of her report to him that Dorrity had been outside his house less than an hour ago. "Come on, folks!" he shouted. "Back to the dance. You haven't even had refreshments yet."

Martha, Jeff, and Burnett did not return to Hayward's, but they urged Janet and Greg to go to represent the guests of honor. Once there, they wished it had been possible to stay away, for they were plied with questions from guests, neighbors, and especially from the Wisnosky youngsters, still drinking pop, to whom a search for buried treasure seemed an open door to riches and romance untold.

"Who is that man with the bulldozer, Janet? What's he goin' t' find? What'll you do with all that money? I bet you won't even be able to stack it all in the barn!"

Greg and Janet answered the questions about the search directly, for there seemed no point now in keeping the matter to themselves. The questions from the older guests about who could have started the fire were soberly asked. Obviously no one felt the fire had been started by a stray cigarette. Few tourists ever wandered back into the private ranch region. The flame must have been deliberately set. Their low aside comments to one another, the puzzled expressions and head shaking, told that these neighbors had suspicions, but did not know upon whom to place them. They probably had not heard of the past troubles the Kaywins had had with Dorrity, and Hayward, Janet, and Greg were careful to say nothing.

The oldest Wisnosky boy was staring at Greg with wistful yearning. He waved a newly emptied bottle of pop. "Sure wisht they'd find gold up there by our house! Why's it have to be just a *mile* away? We could use it."

On the crest of the laughter that followed Hayward changed the subject. "Let's be the only smoked-up people to finish a square dance. Up an' out on the floor, folks!"

By the end of another day, it was apparent that the news was out. Guests from the Lazy O and other dude ranches farther away came to watch. Neighbors could not resist the urge to drive down the side road and watch the proceedings. They did no harm, were careful to follow the fence line down to Burnett's deepening excavation, and stood watching from the pasture side. Even the Wisnosky offspring were careful not to trample the crop that meant cash to ranchers in Jackson Hole. Janet noticed that the Wisnoskys apparently wearied of the scene rather quickly and left after excited whispering among themselves.

For both nights since the fire Jeff, Chuck, and Greg had divided watches among themselves and scouted the borders of Two Rivers. Janet had not told the Kaywins of seeing Dorrity at the Lazy O window. He was already the object of their suspicion and it was possible there was no connection between him and the fire, although she doubted that. She found an old pair of binoculars in a cabinet in the living room and asked if she could use them. At least twice a day she rode or walked to the north end of Two Rivers

and from the low branches of a tree she scouted the Dorrity ranch. With the powerful glasses she spotted the old man usually seated in his front yard staring south toward Two Rivers. He seemed to be what he was not, a harmless old man idling and resting.

Since the fire everybody at Two Rivers had been jittery. Jeff, Chuck, and Greg were losing sleep with their night watches, and were touchy as a result. Janet looked out for Patty and tried to help Martha with the extra work that came about from trying to keep snacks and lunches out for the men operating in shifts.

"I wish that wheat was harvested! I wish that treasure was found! I wish Old Man Dorrity lived someplace else!" Martha exclaimed late the second day. She gave Janet a glance of apology. "I'm jumpy. If things don't get straightened around here, I think I'll fly all over the place."

"I know," Janet told her. "I'm trying not to hope too hard, but it's almost impossible not to."

The bulldozer by now was almost out of sight in the hole Burnett had dug. "Whoever buried that stuff," Burnett seemed so certain something *was* buried there, "put it in the bed of an old stream that apparently has since changed its course. Look at the lay of the land and you can see that there's a depression runs along that fence line. I suppose they thought if it was underwater it was out of reach."

Jeff had risen late the next morning because he had had the last shift of the night before. He walked out on the porch and stretched hugely. Then Martha and Janet heard him shouting.

"Hey you! Get out of that wheat field! What do you think you're doing? Chuck! Greg! Ouch!" Jeff gave a cry of pain from stepping too heavily on his injured leg.

From the kitchen window Janet and Martha saw that a car of ancient vintage had drawn up along the road. All four doors were open and a vanguard of children were scrambling through the fence and racing down through the wheat field toward the excavation. More were pouring out and Janet counted eight before an enormous woman climbed from the front seat and ponderously made for the fence followed by a tall thin slow man.

Some of the brood climbed the wavering, rickety fence. Others rolled under it. The mother took her time unhooking the youngest boy from the fence where he was hung on a barb by the seat of his pants. Then, as though Jeff had not even yelled, she put a heavily shod foot on a rotten fence post, pushed it over, and stepped across the down wires.

Chuck and Greg had been readying the old combine for the wheat harvest, and they came racing from behind the machine shed and took in the situation. "Hey, mister! Get out of that wheat!" Chuck shouted.

The crowd traveled on toward the hole as though they had not even heard. Chuck raced forward in great leaps until he was facing them. "Did you hear? Get your kids out of that wheat!"

The man gave him a look as blank as the flyleaf of a new book. "What wheat?"

"That stuff you're trampin' on is wheat! Get off it!"

"Who says so?"

"I say so!" Chuck yelled. He started toward the visitor, whose wife stepped beside him, and both folded their arms and waited. Meanwhile their children were racing on across the field shouting with excitement.

"Don't waste your time, Chuck!" Burnett yelled. "Let me at 'em!"

He lifted the blade of his bulldozer and ran it rapidly and noisily toward the wheat and the pugnacious couple. At the moment most of the offspring were between the machine and the parents. The woman screamed. Yelling, the children took to their heels and the whole crowd streamed back across the wheat. Bawling insults, they climbed into their automobile and roared away down the road.

Jeff had reached the edge of the field and as Chuck and Greg returned he looked at the paths the trampling feet had made and shook his head. "A few more like that and there'll be no wheat to harvest."

10   *People at Their Worst*

Jeff did not realize how truly he spoke. Fifteen minutes later a car with a Pennsylvania license plate slowed, then parked. A middle-aged couple came strolling leisurely down the fence row. Obviously they knew wheat when they saw it, and they were careful where they put their feet. Openly curious, they plied Jeff with countless questions.

Finally Jeff got a word in. "Where did you hear about this?"

They exchanged a surprised glance. "Why, from the sign down at the pop stand."

"What pop stand?"

"The one down at the corner." The portly tourist thumbed a gesture over his shoulder. "We're just out to see the country so we thought we'd come see what was going on."

"But what does the sign say?"

"It's a sign advertising soft drinks and some kids are running it. There's a painted arrow pointing this way. It says 'Treasure Pop Stand. Watch 'em dig for gold. One-half mile east. Free!'"

Jeff frowned, thinking about this, and the couple, as though sensing their information had not made him happy, turned uncertainly and made their way back up the field to their car without saying good-by. Even as they drove away a station wagon containing a young man with eight boys pulled up. Without so much as a glance at the wheat they trooped across the down fence and streamed across the field toward the excavation.

Jeff slapped his thigh in fury. "Are we going to have to patrol this place? It's not ten o'clock yet. Who are these kids with the pop stand?"

"Let's go see, Dad," Greg suggested.

Minutes later he halted the car at the intersection, and they all stared openmouthed at a patched tent with its front flap raised like an awning to give shade to a tub of ice filled with pop bottles. The tent stood on the very front edge of a yard. The yard, fronting a run-down house, was filled with busy Wisnoskys.

"Wouldn't you know!" Jeff exclaimed.

A tourist car was parked in front of the tent, with several people, dressed for traveling, buying pop. A man pointed at the sign and asked a question and the second Wisnosky boy motioned down the road toward Two Rivers. The oldest boy, who had been working on the other side of the tent, straightened, lifted a piece of cardboard, and went across the road to nail it to a post so that people coming from the other way could also see the directions.

Greg drove up, turned the car around and stopped so they could read the sign. This time the author of the sign had let himself go poetically. STOP FOR POP! THEN SEE THE DIG- GIN'S. IT'S JUST A HOP! Another paint-smeared red arrow pointed the way.

Jeff let out a long amazed breath. "That does it! The first arrow catches all the traffic going up the road through Jackson Hole, and this one catches all of it coming down out of Yellowstone. That'll double the dose we're getting."

Motor idling, they sat watching proceedings. Jackson Hole was experiencing the crest of its tourist season, and cars streamed past them both ways. For every half dozen

that passed, one slowed and turned off the road toward
Two Rivers.

"We've got to get back, or there won't be anything left,"
Jeff said suddenly. "Drive over to that cane-waver, Greg."

Greg had not braked the car before Terry Wisnosky
began crowing. "Hi there, Mr. Kaywin. We're in business!
Made us a buck clear already this mornin'."

Jeff was agitated, but Janet could see him swallowing his
nervousness so that he could speak calmly. "Listen, Terry!
Do you boys realize you're causing us a lot of trouble? All
these people are tramping down our wheat and making a
nuisance of themselves. What'll you take to call off this
deal?" He pointed at the red arrow.

The oldest Wisnosky child was quite prepared to take
care of such interruptions as this in his own way.
"Nothin'!" he retorted. "We're in business sellin' pop just
so long's you Kaywins are in the business of diggin' fer
treasure."

Jeff's face reddened, and his mouth tightened with anger.
"In that case, I'll have to take care of the matter of putting
up private signs on a public highway myself."

Easing himself out of the back seat of the car, Jeff limped
toward the red arrow. Terry Wisnosky watched him half-

way across the intervening distance. "Pop!" he called.

As though he had been waiting for the call, a shambling overall-clad man with long mustaches partially concealing a cadaverous face stepped out on the porch. He carried a shotgun. "Let that thar sign alone, Mr. Kaywin."

Jeff limped on, speaking over his shoulder. "That sign, George, is spoiling a year's profit for me. I'm taking it down."

The voice from the porch was as quiet as though it mentioned the weather. If anything, it had dropped to a lower and more ominous range. "I said—leave it alone. That sign ain't on no public highway. It's in my yard. The one acrost the road's on a post of my pasture. Touch either an' I'll shoot yuh or have you arrested or both."

Greg had leaped from the car. "Dad! Come back!"

Jeff had stopped. He looked from the sign to George Wisnosky who had lifted his gun now, carrying it tucked under his elbow so that a mere gesture could bring it to position. Lips tight, Jeff stood his ground, returning Wisnosky's stare.

"I mean it, mister," George told him deliberately. "Man disturbs what belongs to me, I'd as leave shoot him as not. If it pleases you, go to the sheriff. I'll tell him you disturbed my property. You ranchers 'round these parts think you got it all your way. George Wisnosky ain't got much, but he knows what he's got comin' from the law, an' mister, don't you fergit it!"

"Come on back, Dad," Greg urged. His voice was as low and quiet as Wisnosky's own, but Janet, poker-stiff on the front seat, could almost feel the faint quaver of it.

Jeff knew defeat when he saw it. He twisted on his good foot, returned to the car, and indicated that Greg should drive on. When Greg turned into the side road that led to Two Rivers, he followed three cars which, considering that the road was a dead end at the ranch, could only be going there. The three of them did not exchange a word on the way home. When they arrived a dozen cars were parked along the wheat field. Chuck, working alone, was trying to keep people along the fence line. Some obeyed his directions, but others seemed not even to see him.

Jeff made his only comment. "Well, kids, looks as though all we can do is protect what's ours, same as he does. Spread out along what used to be the fence."

Janet looked at the wheat field. Already paths were run down through it, golden heads trampled under uncaring feet. The wheat was not ruined, not yet, but it would not take much more. She hurried down along the edge of the field to take her stand a hundred feet beyond Greg, and with Chuck beyond her. From where she stood she could see that the excavation now showed only Burnett's head above his machine. Around the edge of the hole the dirt had been piled high. People stood or sat on the pile, twenty or thirty of them, and watched, while their children, tiring soon of the sight of a hole with a bulldozer in it, raced out through the field or into the pasture. Janet caught a five-year-old as he tore past her with a small girl chasing him. She snatched the girl when the child ran headlong into her. With a firm hand on each arm she marched them down to the fence line and then to the hole.

"Whom do these kids belong to?" she demanded.

A woman turned with a vague glance. "What's wrong with 'em, miss? They're just playin' tag."

"That's for sure," Janet told her, "and in a private wheat field. You're on private property and if you don't keep them out of the crop, I'll lock them in the icehouse until you leave."

Muttering, the father gathered his progeny and marched off indignantly, the mother casting vague glances back at Janet as though wondering what had motivated such action.

The sun was at noon now, and the weather had turned hot. The cars passing churned up dust on the wind. Janet could feel it on her skin and in her hair. Between the four of them now they were doing a creditable job of keeping people along the fence, but even so, some refused to be directed.

"Young lady," one burly man said severely, "that sign you've got back at the highway says this is free, an' I'm goin' to see it. Try an' stop me." He walked straight across the field.

He strode forward as though to walk right over her. Janet stood her ground and pointed down toward the fence line fifty feet distant. "That's the way."

He was almost on her now, and Jeff yelled sharply. "Mister, go where you're supposed to or get out!"

The burly man halted, muttering uncertainly. Jeff limped toward him and the man backed away, then returned to his car, casting black looks over his shoulder. Jeff started to return to his post, but as he did so Janet saw that his face under its tan was pale. Then he staggered.

"Greg!" Janet shouted as she rushed to him. They caught and held him upright, and Jeff, with a moist, shaking hand, mopped his face.

"Get to the house, Dad," Greg urged. "You haven't been standing this long at a time before or in this heat. Here, I'll take you in."

There was a noon-hour lull, and one at a time the three guards took twenty minutes apiece to go to the house and eat. Janet found Jeff lying across the bed looking exhausted. Martha was readying meals for the family and fuming.

"I never knew people could be like this! Look what it's done to Jeff! Look at that wheat field!"

Burnett came up as Janet went out the door. "A hole in the ground, and everybody has to come look at it! I've seen it happen before."

"You should have warned us!" Martha said wearily.

"If there was a place I could have begun digging that I'd have thought nobody'd find, I'd have said this was it," Burnett told her. "It didn't seem necessary."

Afternoon brought the full peak of the crowd. Again it was the same experience as the morning had been, but intensified. Two-thirds of the people followed directions. The remainder, because the sight was free and available, were going to go where they wished and do as they pleased, and they were not going to be stopped by a teen-age boy, a girl, and one ranch hand. Some, stopped by the three

guards along the road, merely went back to cut around through the wheat where there was no one to keep them out; others went ahead and cut through the pasture, or even into the timber and came down through the house yard.

The Kaywins that afternoon saw human nature at its bad-mannered worst. Once they heard Martha scream, and looking over their shoulders in alarm, they saw Martha driving a woman and a small boy out of her house with the broom.

Janet, frustrated, angry, and tired, finally burst into tears as she looked out over the trampled wheat. A woman, coming back through, passed her a half-filled bottle of pop, probably purchased at the Wisnosky stand. "Here, honey, you're tired. Take this. You oughta get outa that sun. You'll get burned!"

Chuck broke into a loud snicker in spite of his annoyance as Janet backed away in disgust. "Git along, lady. She's already burned, but it ain't sun, it's humanity done it. Git!"

On the other hand, one slim youth in Western clothes saw what was happening, waved Chuck farther on down the fence line and guarded a portion himself for more than an hour.

"Got to go get my kid," he explained finally as he went to his car. Dusty, disheveled, but cheerful, he was gone before anyone even found out his name.

By late afternoon the crowd was mostly gone. "Let's quit," Chuck said. "We should have quit sooner. It was no use." His gaze combed the wheat field, runneled with paths, trampled for a hundred feet out from the excavation. Wearily they went toward the house. Down in the hole Burnett worked on, so intent on his job that he did not even see them pass.

Janet took a pitcher of hot water to her room. It seemed to her that she barely had strength enough left to pour it into the bowl on the washstand. More than anything in the world she wanted to drop across the bed and sleep, but she made herself bathe and put on clean clothes.

When she went downstairs, Greg, Chuck, and Martha were sitting on the porch steps staring out at the wheat. Jeff limped out a moment after Janet had come. Suddenly Martha dropped her head in her hands. "I never dreamed people could be like that! It's all my fault. I wanted to try this, but all I've done is made us lose Two Rivers! One more day and there won't be a thing left of that field."

Jeff laid a hand on her shoulder as she wept soundlessly,

a depth of grief the more pitiful because it was terribly real and nothing any of them could change.

There was a sound of many hoofs trotting into the yard, and they turned to see Hayward and several of his guests on horseback. "Jeff, we've been away all day and just now saw what's been going on in your wheat field!"

His glance traveled from Jeff to Martha, drying her tears with her back to him, on to the glum faces of Greg and Chuck, and to Janet.

Jeff filled him in on the day's experiences, beginning with the Wisnosky family and ending with the Kaywin failure to turn the tide of determined humanity off Two Rivers. "Looks as though we're washed up," he finished. "I counted on that wheat to make my mortgage payment."

Janet watched one lone visitor stride across the field in the twilight, and suddenly she was angry. "Isn't there any fence around? Something we could put up before morning? I wish we could make people pay for what they've done!"

Hayward had moved his white-socked gelding a few paces ahead for a closer look, and he sat looking as Jeff answered. "How you going to make 'em pay? The sight's free. That's why they come."

Hayward twisted suddenly in the saddle, his glance

going from Jeff to Janet. "Hey, wait a minute! Between the two of you, you said it!"

"Said what?" Martha asked.

"Free. Fence. Make 'em pay. Jeff, you got any electric fencing?"

"One length," Jeff told him. "Old and on a dead battery."

"I've got two, and we can borrow some," Hayward said. "Jeff, the girl's idea is sound. People only value what they have to pay to see."

"People wouldn't pay." Jeff's reply was scornful.

"Why not?" Hayward demanded. Behind him a couple of his riders edged their horses closer. "In Missouri where I was raised everybody with a half-pint cave on his farm advertises a trip through it for a quarter. You'd be surprised at the people who stop and go through."

Greg had risen to his feet. The slack, discouraged lines in Martha's face were tightening with excitement. Janet felt her spirits rise. "Mr. Hayward, do you really think it might work?"

"Young lady, your idea is worth a try anyhow. I feel a little responsible for this mess, Jeff. If it hadn't been for your project getting announced at my dance, you probably wouldn't be where you are."

He wheeled Piper around. "You folks look plumb tuckered. Get a couple hours' rest and I'll be back."

Inside Janet helped Martha get the meal on the table. Supper was eaten in silence, for everyone seemed to be thinking. The atmosphere had lost its feeling of discouragement, yet nobody quite believed matters could improve.

Hayward and four of his summer visitors were back in less than two hours. The back of his pickup truck was filled with rolls of wire and a pile of steel fence posts. "Been to Jackson. Implement Company there says use the posts and return 'em. Same with the wire. Come on, boys."

Martha and Janet did not let the word *boys* stop them. The moon was rising when they reached the fence row. The two women rolled the wire spools the length of the field while the men began driving the posts. New vigor had seized Jeff, Chuck, and Greg. At least, this was attacking the problem instead of being defeated by it.

"How many wires will you put up?" Janet asked Hayward.

"Six strands, and to a height of five feet. Close enough to the ground so they can't roll under and high enough so they can't climb it. If they try either one they'll get bitten."

In two hours the fence was finished. "Now sandwiches and coffee in the kitchen," Martha told them.

As Hayward went out the door an hour later, he turned. "Janet, paint us about three signs to hang on the posts reading 'Charged Fence.' We have to be legal about this and warn people so nobody gets shocked and can say he didn't know it was electric fencing. We'll be down in the morning and give you a hand for the day, and on the way I'll tell the Wisnoskys to take down that 'Free' sign they have up."

"We probably won't have any visitors then," Jeff said.

"Bet you have twice as many," Hayward told him.

11 *A Case of Sorehead*

Janet had the signs hung by eight o'clock the next morning. By nine cars were coming. "We'll try you out as gatekeeper," Hayward told Janet. "What are you going to charge?"

"A dollar apiece," Janet said promptly, studying the ruined wheat field, which looked worse by daylight than it had at dusk yesterday.

Hayward shouted with laughter. "Then Jeff will be right. We'll have no visitors. Better settle for a quarter apiece. But see that they pay. People feel better, really, paying for what they get. Here come your first customers. I'll go tell Terry to take down that 'Free' sign."

Twenty minutes later he returned laughing. "Yesterday

George Wisnosky was sore because Jeff tried to stop his business. Today he's sore because *we're* charging. I told him if he kept up that 'Free' sign I'd have to tell the sheriff he was misrepresenting our business. He was happy then to settle for having you paint him a new sign saying, 'Twenty-five cents admission.'"

Janet painted the new sign and rode down on Sawdust to deliver it. Together she and Terry backed off to admire her handiwork. "Gee, it looks real elegant!" Terry exclaimed. "I ain't good at paintin'. How about some pop signs?"

Janet agreed, feeling that she had connived with the enemy and unexpectedly found him a saint. As she galloped home, cars were thick on the way to the "diggin'." In the dust Greg was making change from the carpenter's apron he had found. Now and then the battery-wired fence clicked faintly. Once Greg, during a lull, ran his hands through the coins in the apron; he turned to glance over the wheat field, then looked at Janet and shrugged. The wheat field was not quite the issue it had been.

At the house Patty was sitting idly on the porch steps, glumly staring at the scene she had been told to avoid. "Play with me, Jan—et!"

"Honey, wait until things let up a little. I have to make Terry another sign." Before this began she had often played with Patty, teaching her to play hopscotch and to bat a small rubber ball. Now Patty was lonesome. Martha was much too busy to play with her, and today Jeff had to stay in bed.

The signs delivered, Janet spelled Greg at the gate. A steady stream of humanity was paying without complaint to see a hole in the ground. Hayward had been right: People felt better paying for what they got. The three-foot embankment was lined with people watching anxiously to see if the next blade-load would reveal a treasure.

Burnett paid them no attention. Janet had never seen a man work with such concentration. Having dug the surface away, he now was handling the bulldozer as delicately as a woman picking up two threads of a dress hem. He took off no more than half an inch at a time, studied the surface, wheeled his machine, and repeated the operation.

Greg became impatient. "Why don't you bite in deeper?"

Burnett looked up. "What I find will probably be within the next two feet. I wouldn't want to ruin it, for it could be the difference between a fortune and nothing. As I said, I've two weeks to spend, and it doesn't matter if I use every minute of it so long's I find what I want. The Geiger counter still shows something's there."

"What will we do with that hole when he's gone?" Martha asked when Burnett had returned to work another hour with the machine he now was leaving in the hole nights.

"Maybe we can pipe in the spring on the other side of the pasture and have ourselves a swimming pool," Greg told her brightly. "What you're really saying, Mom, is that you don't think Mr. Burnett's going to find anything."

Martha pulled at her lip thoughtfully. "I still can't think he'd put in all these hours, two weeks of time, if something wasn't there."

Jeff had come out to supper in pajamas and robe. "What it probably adds up to is that in two weeks we'll have a swimmin' hole two feet deeper than it would be if he quit right now."

His tone was glum and Martha sighed. To change the subject Greg went to the living room and returned with the carpenter's apron he had used all day. Pushing back plates and glasses, he upended the apron and spilled coins and bills in a silver-and-green cascade onto the tablecloth. Jeff leaned forward, an expression of astonishment on his face. Martha's mouth popped open, and after a silent moment she put out her hand and slowly touched the pile as though she could not quite believe it.

"Is it real?" she asked faintly. "Real money?"

"It's real enough," Greg told her. "Janet and I stood out there and took it in all day. There's not enough to pay for the wheat but give a week and there will be. Let's count it."

Martha separated the bills while Jeff took the quarters and the rest separated nickels from dimes. When the assortment was in separate stacks, they began counting and adding.

"One hundred and ninety dollars," Jeff breathed. "Just to look at a hole in the ground."

"Once during a lull I counted the people around the hole. There were almost two hundred," Janet told him.

Jeff leaned back. "Now I don't care how long he digs! All I hope is that he doesn't have to quit."

The next morning Janet had to reflect that Jeff's casual remarks had a way of anticipating the immediate future. Burnett returned to the house half an hour after leaving for work. His lips were tight with anger. "Somebody did us in!"

"What happened?" Martha cried.

"Couldn't start the bulldozer. The wires are all torn loose and the radiator looks as though somebody had smashed it in with a hammer."

They were silent in the face of the disaster. "What will you do?" Jeff asked finally.

"I'll leave now for repairs. Jackson doesn't carry a line of bulldozer repairs and the break in the radiator is too bad for soldering. I'll have to buy a whole new radiator, and that means a fifty-mile trip downstate to get it." He took his car keys off a shelf by the kitchen door and started out. "Watch that machine while I'm gone. From now on we put out a guard nights."

"Were there any tracks you could see?"

"There were tracks but somebody had tried to brush 'em out by dragging a branch behind him. Anyway, it would be hard to tell because he wore moccasins and the prints hardly show. It was a small foot for a man."

In fairness, Janet told the people who came to the gate the next day that there was little to see because somebody had sabotaged the machinery during the night. Business was less, but even so a few paid the fee and looked anyhow.

Terry Wisnosky, however, heard about the delay and came down to investigate. "So what?" he demanded. "Quit turnin' 'em away. Make somethin' of it."

Within an hour after he left, the crowds were coming as before. "I hear you had trouble last night," one visitor commented. "Thought I'd have a look."

Plenty of people had a look that day. Even Jeff had to laugh. "I bet that Wisnosky kid makes a million before he's through with his ideas," he remarked. "Hayward tells me he added the word 'Sabotage' above the signs he already had up. It's a good thing for Terry that the crowd of tourists is different every day or he'd never get away with it."

Burnett returned late that day and spent part of the night putting new parts on his machine with Greg holding a flashlight for him. He finished at one o'clock in the morning, came to the house and wakened Chuck, who had volunteered to stand guard on the machine the rest of the night.

At ten the next morning Terry was back. He was making an almost daily check on what went on at Two Rivers now in order to change his business tactics whenever necessary. At the excavation Burnett had stopped his machine to put in gas. Terry took immediate advantage of the interval of quiet. "Hey, Mr. Burnett, when you goin' to uncover that treasure, anyway? Pretty soon now?"

Burnett straightened, grinned as he flexed weary arms and shoulders. "Oh, give me *one* more day! Just one!"

Terry turned away, headed for home, and as he passed Janet he gave her a broad, meaning wink. By noon the crowds began to increase and by two o'clock in the afternoon the intake of quarters at the turnstile was a steady jingle in the apron. Greg, Chuck, and Janet were spelling each other off in two-hour shifts, and as Greg finished his during early afternoon, he turned to Janet just coming on for the second time that day. "I'm going to ride Charcoal down to the corner and see what Terry's done now that picked up business so fast."

Patty had followed Janet down to the gate so she could walk back with Greg. "Greg, take me with you. I want to go see, too."

"Can't, Pat," Greg told her. "I'm riding Charcoal, and you can't ride. Especially not Char."

Patty was pouting as she trotted after Greg's long strides. Later when Greg had gone Janet turned to see the child in the distance sitting in her usual place on the top porch step.

Greg returned in a little while. "Leave it to Terry! He's

got a new sign, bigger than the others, under the one about coming to see the diggings. It says, 'Treasure any minute now!' I bought a bottle of pop and listened to his sales spiel. He's got a regular sales talk about the deal down here, and of course he always adds that the man doing the digging says, 'One more day now.' That one's good for next day every day. Well, I'm going to go eat so I can gather strength for this business after you."

"I'd love to take a short ride when I'm through," Janet told him. "How about bringing Sawdust down here so I can grab a quickie when you relieve me?"

She did not take the time to add that her duties had kept her from checking on what Dorrity was doing these days, and that after the sabotage of the bulldozer it was time somebody watched.

"Will do," Greg replied.

Janet had been at work perhaps half an hour when a scream came from the house and the pounding of hoofs cut through the roar of the bulldozer. She whirled to see Charcoal racing out of the yard, and hanging to the saddle was Patty. Martha was running in a desperate effort to cut the horse off, and Greg and Chuck were racing around the corner of the barn.

Janet flung off her apron as she left the gate and rushed to Sawdust, remembering as she threw the reins over his neck that Greg had left Charcoal tied to the corral fence when he had saddled and brought Sawdust down for her.

She swung to the saddle, hearing the excited screams of watchers at the hole as the black horse tore past on the other side of the pasture and headed at a run up the road toward Pacific Creek. She struck the old palomino with the rein ends and hammered his ribs as she sent him full speed directly through the timber in an attempt to intercept the black. She had galloped rapidly but she had never put Sawdust to full speed, and now with a snort the horse responded with a burst of speed that blurred the passing landscape and filled her eyes with tears. Sawdust plunged over logs and crashed through bushes, and Janet, intent on Patty, forgot to cling to the horn of the saddle.

Then Sawdust, in mid-air, shied suddenly, and she felt herself slipping. Half out of the saddle, she grabbed the pommel and clung desperately, aware that behind the log over which Sawdust had jumped as he shied, a hunched, bearded figure had crouched. The figure of Dorrity, a pair of field glasses in his hand, was as clear in her mind as though she had been sitting in a chair to watch it.

Feeling his burden off-center, Sawdust slowed uncertainly, and the pause gave Janet time to haul herself back into the saddle and send him flying on. The pause, however, had given the black time to clear the bend close to Pacific Creek before she could reach the road to head him off. Charcoal, with Patty still clinging desperately but managing to stay in the saddle, was half a block ahead of her when she came out of the timber onto the trail.

Then with horror Janet remembered that Dorrity had shut off the trail at Pacific Creek. What would Charcoal do? Jump the fence, crash into it, or wheel away from it so suddenly Patty would be thrown? The thought of Patty's small body flying over the fence into Pacific Creek or, worse yet, being knocked into the barbs of the fence made Janet sick with fear.

Charcoal knew barbed wire. Fifty feet before the fence he slowed, trotted to it, paused a moment, then turned and came galloping back. Janet wheeled Sawdust squarely into his path, and the palomino, old cow horse that he was, saw a job coming up. As the black dodged toward the Dorrity fence, he wheeled in front of him there, and when Charcoal tried to cut around on the timber side, he leaped in front and close enough so Janet could reach down and seize the dangling broken rein. For a moment the two horses were spinning round and round together, with Sawdust, his ears flat, crowding against Charcoal to stop him.

Patty was sobbing. "Ja—Ja—net, g-get me off!"

Still holding Charcoal close, Janet leaned over. "Put your arms around my neck and hang on when I pull back so you can come over on Sawdust."

"No! No, Jan—et, I want down!"

The thought came to Janet that Patty all this summer had wanted to ride. Now she had backed a horse too much for her, and if permitted to walk home, she probably would never let herself know the fun of riding a horse. Without a pause, Janet gathered all the reins in her left hand and with her right she reached out and scooped Patty off Charcoal and set her before her in the saddle.

"There you are! Sawdust won't hurt you."

The pounding of feet was coming down the trail. That would be Greg and Martha. Janet touched Sawdust with her heels, and leading Charcoal, they set out to meet them. Patty's face was tear-stained, her breath came in short hiccups; her small, trembling body was still stiff with fright.

"Here, Patty, I'll slide behind the saddle and lead Charcoal and you take the reins and guide Sawdust. You show

Mamma you can do it." Hastily Janet pulled out a handker-chief and wiped Patty's face. "Don't let anybody see you're scared. Sawdust won't run unless you make him. Tell Mamma you want to ride him home."

Hurriedly then Janet lifted her legs, turned backward on Sawdust's rump and slid to the ground over his tail, leaving Patty riding a horse alone. As Greg came panting around the bend in the trail, Janet waved him down, put a finger to her lips, and pointed to his sister who was already beginning to control her sobs. Clinging to the horn with one hand, Patty reached out and gingerly picked up the reins with the other. All the pull she could put on them would not have stopped Sawdust or any other horse, but as though he understood the situation perfectly, the reliable old horse plodded quietly on down the road toward home.

Martha ran up, her breath coming in gasps. "Oh, Patty, get off that horse! Why did you—?"

Greg, walking in the lead, spoke in a low tone, his hand out. "Wait, Mom. Pat just picked the wrong nag. Sawdust won't hurt her. Let her ride."

Her mother's objections were all it took to convince Patty she should ride home. Her hand, still a little shaky, but also determined, reached out to pat Sawdust's withers. "Let me,

Mamma. He's a nice horse. I want to ride him home."

Sawdust, being as helpful as possible, made the decision for Martha. Ignoring them all, he walked on down the road so that they followed in his wake.

Martha let out a tremulous sigh, and Janet, for a different reason, let out another as she handed Charcoal's broken reins to Greg. Within the past ten minutes an ambition had been achieved and a suspicion confirmed. Patty had ridden a horse and Old Man Dorrity was watching what went on at Two Rivers. Catching Greg's sleeve she slowed him to fall behind Martha, who was keeping close to Patty. She had to tell him about seeing Dorrity behind the log.

Greg investigated the spot, but all he found was trampled grass.

Janet, dead tired, was in bed before twilight faded. She was sufficiently weary to have slept through until morning. Instead, she awoke sometime before dawn without the numbing drowsiness a sleeper usually feels. She lay listening intently. A night bird cheeped monotonously; bullfrogs croaked from the pasture stream. Then the night bird ceased and so did the bullfrogs. Janet sat up in bed and pushed back the covers. The floor was cold on her bare feet as she moved to the window and stared out toward the pit where

Greg would be standing guard. The night was completely dark, completely silent, as though everything waited—and something threatened.

Then she heard a scrambling sound. There was a clang of metal, and a boy's voice cried out in pain. Janet wheeled and raced down the hallway from her room, hammering on Chuck's door as she passed, calling to Martha and Jeff as she flew downstairs.

Their pajama-clad forms hurried into the kitchen as she lit the lamp with shaking hands. "I heard Greg yell! Something's wrong!"

Martha snatched the flashlight from the shelf and rushed out the door ahead of Jeff, Chuck, and Burnett. By the time Janet arrived she was casting the beam out over the pit as the men hurried into its depths.

At first no one saw anything. "Greg!" Jeff called. "Greg?"

Then Chuck called from behind the bulldozer. "Here he is! Bring the light!"

Janet caught up the flashlight and turned it on the prone form of Greg as Martha dropped down beside him. "Oh, Greg!"

"Don't lift him, Mrs. Kaywin! Not yet," Chuck warned

her. "Here, let me . . . ." He bent over the boy.

Janet remembered then that Chuck had been an ambulance driver in World War II. He ran expert hands over Greg's back and neck, legs and arms. When his exploring fingers came to Greg's head, they came away bloody. Martha's breath sucked in fearfully.

"His bones are all right," Chuck said. "He's been knocked out. Let's get him to the house."

His short, powerful frame bent, lifted, straightened, as Martha hurried ahead to get the bed ready and Janet lighted the way up the incline. Martha had water and cloth ready by the time Chuck laid Greg on the bed. The boy moaned as Martha pressed a cold cloth to his head wound.

"Comin' around," Chuck muttered. "Give him time!"

Finally Greg's eyelids fluttered, but it was fifteen minutes before he could speak. He was groggy and his expression was alternately pained and puzzled.

"Wha—what happened?" he asked.

"Don't talk till you feel like it, boy," Chuck told him.

Finally Greg's expression cleared. "I—remember. I tackled something in the dark. Must . . ." For a moment his face was again blank. "Must've been a gorilla."

Half an hour later he could tell them what had occurred

at the pit. "I heard something coming across the pasture. Then I saw it outlined against the sky on the edge of the pit before it came down."

"What was it, son?" Jeff asked.

Greg frowned. "I don't know. It was just a big, humped shape. When it was close enough I jumped on it thinking I could catch whoever was damaging the machine. But I couldn't hold onto him. It was a man—could have been Old Man Dorrity—but he was wrapped in a blanket or something. When I jumped on his back and grabbed him around the neck he twisted and hit me. Not with his fist. He must've carried a wrench or something. Did he hurt the machine?"

Burnett, who had been standing at the foot of the bed, was out of the house in a flash. He had completely forgotten his beloved bulldozer.

"No damage," he reported fifteen minutes later. "Thanks to you!"

When Greg had been put to bed and told to stay there all the next day, the rest of them lingered in the kitchen, and for the first time Janet noticed that Patty was standing on the bottom step of the stairs.

"We woke you up, didn't we, Patty?" Janet said, extending a hand to the sober little girl. "Greg's all right. We're going back to bed now. Come on."

Patty's sense of outrage over the past week's neglect was not to be so easily appeased. She avoided the hand. "No. It's all that awful Mr. Dorrity's fault. If he hadn't made Mr. Burnett come here, everybody would play with me like they used to. We wouldn't have lost the wheat. Greg wouldn't have got his head hurt. And I could ride Sawdust."

As Patty turned and went upstairs with her head loftily high, Janet looked questioningly at Martha, who sighed with exasperation. "I told her she couldn't ride Sawdust unless somebody was with her. Despite her experience with Charcoal, she thinks she can ride like a Comanche because she rode that gentle horse home at a walk!"

From the head of the stairs Patty had turned to look down on them. "It's Mr. Dorrity's fault!" she repeated emphatically. "And I'm going to tell him so, too!"

Her pink flannel nightgown whipped around the corner into her own room. Chuck whistled. "Whew! Has she got a case of sorehead! I'm not so sure she's not right, too."

12   *"If It Weren't for You—"*

The next few days were hot and windy, long and tiring. In the course of them the Kaywin household lost the sense of excitement and anticipation that had held them in its grip. During the first week of Burnett's project their hours of hope had offset their hours of doubt, but now all that was left was a feeling of letdown and a conviction that they were still committed to a week of ridiculous and useless treasure hunting.

At breakfast when everyone except Burnett, already out at work, was present, Martha expressed the feeling of all, her words coming out on the crest of a quick, sharp sigh.

"Only five more days and I'm glad. I've had enough! I don't know what we'll do for money this winter, but I think we can live without it easier than we can keep on earning it this way. We've been overrun with tourists, covered with dust, hit on the head, and snowed under with work . . . all for a hole in the ground and enough shekels to almost, but not quite, pay for the wheat."

Chuck was the only one with enough energy left to muster a grin. Jeff nodded grimly, and Janet and Greg remained silent. The only ones who had not yet had enough of treasure digging were the tourists.

Each evening Jeff checked the market price of wheat that day against the additional gate intake. "Closer," he would remark. "Keep the gate going. That's our only chance."

That evening remark served to keep them all on the routine. The shifts for Janet, Jeff, and Greg were longer now because Chuck was trying to pick up what remained of the wheat with a combine he was having trouble keeping together. Janet took the shift from nine until twelve, Greg from noon until three in the afternoon, and Jeff finished during the interval when the day was cooling down.

No rain had come for some time, and the road was ankle-deep in dust that blew in the wind in brief gusts. Dust devils filled Janet's hair and clothing with grit. She could taste it and feel it between her teeth. By eleven the day had turned hot and the sun beat down so that her head hurt and her eyeballs ached with the glare. During brief lulls between cars she often found herself standing with her eyes closed against the brilliance and thinking of the summer back-yard ball games at home, and of her family. When she had been relieved and had rested a few minutes, she usually saddled Sawdust, rode briefly south, then cut back through the forest until she came to the Dorrity-Kaywin boundary fence. There, screened by the timber, she stared at the old man's cabin until she had located him. Most of his time he spent sitting in an old rocker on his porch, staring south.

"He doesn't do a thing but sit there," she told Greg.

"Maybe the old boy's pouting because I jumped him that night," Greg answered. He touched a hand to the spot just under his hat brim where a bandage showed. "So am I!"

One day Patty came to where Janet was saddling up. "Can't I go with you, Jan—et? I want to ride."

Janet hesitated, "Go ask Mamma, Patty."

Patty returned in a few moments. "She says I can't. She says she isn't going to have to worry about me until she hasn't got anything else to worry about."

That, Janet thought, would probably be quite a while. She mounted. "As soon as Mr. Burnett's through I'll talk to Mamma, Patty. We won't have so much to do then, and she'll probably let you ride. Just be patient."

Patty burst into tears. "I want to ride *now!*"

Janet almost yielded to the desire to pull the little girl up behind her on Sawdust, but she knew she had no right to go against Martha's orders. "You'll have to wait, Patty. I can't let you ride unless Mamma says so."

The week was into its third day when Janet, half asleep standing at the turnstile, became aware that Chuck had called to her. She turned to see him dogtrotting across the field toward the excavation. He glanced back over his shoulder gesturing her to come, and she latched the turnstile and started after him, aware that Burnett was nowhere in sight, the machine was shut off, and that the watchers were leaning forward, staring down with some excitement.

When she reached the pit Burnett was down in front of the bulldozer, his fingers exploring what appeared to be a corner of a metal box. The blade of the machine had torn into the corner, but the hole was too small to let light inside.

Burnett glanced up as Chuck and Janet dropped down

beside him. His glance was as pleasantly serious as always. "Time to start spade work now."

They notified Greg, Martha, and Jeff. Returning with spades, they began digging, under Burnett's direction, around the box. "Don't punch into the box. Just clear away the dirt."

Martha and Jeff kept the crowd back, and the three men worked until the old metal box, perhaps two feet long and a foot wide, rested on a short pedestal of earth under it. It was ancient looking with brassbound corners, and locked.

As Burnett slowly forced the lid back on its hinges, Janet found herself hardly breathing. Everyone was silent now. Jeff stared at the chest as though hypnotized. Martha, her hands held tensely to each side of her face, had an unbelieving look in her eyes. Then the lid squealed and broke off as Burnett kept pushing it, and gasps went up from the watchers. The box was filled almost to the top with oddly shaped black blocks such as Janet had never seen before.

"Ingots," Burnett said softly. He reached out and lifted one, turning it carefully in his hands. Obviously it was heavy. He reached into his pocket for his penknife and scratched on the bar. The black tarnish of years, of centuries, scraped away and revealed silvery brightness underneath.

"Silver!" he said softly. "What do you know! Ingots of solid silver."

Slowly Martha's hands came away from her cheeks and she looked at Jeff, who let out a slow breath. Janet found her fists had been doubled until they hurt, and she began working her fingers.

Then the moment was broken as Burnett rose briskly to his feet. "Well, how about the gate receipts, Mr. Kaywin? Break even on the wheat?"

Jeff swallowed in surprise. This was the first time Burnett had taken the least interest in anything at Two Rivers besides the hunt and his bulldozer. "The—the gate receipts plus what was left of the wheat would almost have equaled what the wheat would have made otherwise. I'd hoped to pay off a little of the principal on my mortgage this year."

"You just have, Mr. Kaywin. You have done just that," Burnett assured him. "Uncle Sam pays by the ounce for pure silver, and there's a lot of ounces in that box, maybe twenty thousand dollars' worth."

He pulled an old envelope from his shirt pocket and scribbled on it, then handed it to Jeff. "Send this telegram for me, will you? This man is a museum representative and a friend of mine. I want him here."

Herbert Duvall of a Cleveland museum arrived by air within a few hours. He was a small, delicately built man with prematurely white hair and a tiny Vandyke beard. Although he looked completely out of place in overalls, he went to work in the pit with enthusiasm.

Within the next three days four chests were found. They lay perhaps six feet apart, and a length of rusted chain ran from one to the other, not fastened to the chests, but linked to iron collars that had been locked apparently with keys.

"Slave collars," Duvall explained. "Slaves were killed where they set the boxes down and buried with them so they'd never be able to tell where this stuff was buried."

"How do you know?" Janet asked him. "There's nothing there but the chests and chains."

"After three or four hundred years, no. Not even bones. But we museum men have seen enough of this sort of thing to know what those locked collars mean. Slaves were expendable."

Two of the three remaining chests also contained ingots, but the fourth held a single richly carved urn, which Burnett lifted from its resting place with reverent hands.

Duvall's eyes glowed. "Spanish silver, and—" he frowned in deep thought, "I'd guess it's the work of a certain famous silversmith of four hundred years ago in Spain. We've never found much of his stuff. I won't even clean it until it reaches the museum where we've got the equipment."

Duvall had taken an option to buy the urn for the museum at a price to be set by a staff committee. "I know it will never be less than thirty thousand dollars," he assured them. Astonishment left Martha and Jeff speechless, and even Burnett looked a bit dazed. The ingots were put in a vault at the bank at Jackson to await a Government representative.

"Three boxes of ingots times twenty thousand dollars each. Plus the urn." Martha was multiplying on her fingers. Her mouth dropped open at the result.

"What are you going to do with it?" Jeff teased her.

Martha had immediate answers. "Pay off the mortgage. Put in electricity. Get a new combine. Fix up this kitchen. Buy a new stove." Suddenly she laughed a little hysterically and gave the old cook stove a little kick. "Just imagine not having to have a morning hassle with you any more!"

For the Kaywins it was a time of unbelievable satisfaction. Chuck forgot the combine and the wheat; they let Terry Wisnosky take over the turnstile. All of them, curious, bemused, and awed, seemed to be able to do nothing but sit on the bank with the tourists and watch Burnett and Duvall dig to see if anything more was to be found. That is, all of them did except Patty. For ten days she had not been permitted to go near the hole unless someone was with her. Now that the whole family was there most of the time, she sat on the back steps and watched from a distance, refusing to have anything to do with the whole business.

Janet, sitting beside Martha one afternoon, was conscious that Martha was staring toward the house. "You know," Martha remarked, "I haven't seen Patty for an hour. She was on the porch with that old doll she resurrected yesterday."

"Sit still," Janet told her. "I'll find her."

The child was not in the house, the yard, or around the barns. Greg had ridden Charcoal to a neighbor's ranch to help with some cattle and Sawdust grazed alone at the other end of the pasture. Janet set off down the lane, thinking Patty might have taken a stroll, and was relieved to find small sandal tracks in the dust.

A quarter of a mile from the house the tracks turned left into the woods and now and then Janet could see where the youngster had stepped on soft earth or sand. She started to hurry now; even natives got lost in Jackson Hole country and Patty rarely got far from the house. The tracks crossed a small stream once and appeared thereafter to be circling toward the house, but a quarter of a mile from the excavation, she found a piece of the yellow facial tissue which Patty had used to dress the doll.

Patty, however, was not with the crowd at the hole, and Janet, without worrying Martha, went on, expecting at any moment to catch up with the child. She discovered now that Patty was not circling, she was making a straight line north.

Suddenly Janet stopped. "Oh, no!" she whispered. What was it Patty had said the night Greg was hurt? *It's all Mr. Dorrity's fault and I'm going to tell him so!*

Then she was running. She paused only once, when she saw the old doll lying beside the Dorrity fence. Minutes later she was panting beside the ledge where once she had watched for the dogs. As she rubbed a sleeve across her sweating face and parted the blackberry bushes, she had a glimpse of Dorrity that she would never forget. He was standing in front of his old rocker on the porch and in the chair was Patty. Her feet did not reach the floor, and her small frame, shrinking from Dorrity, seemed lost in the big rocker. Dorrity, foot on the step, was leaning toward her, and in Patty's bloodless, saucer-eyed face was the knowledge that she had attempted more than she could handle. She stared up at him like a snake-terrified bird.

Janet could not hear what Dorrity was saying, but he leaned forward and patted Patty on the head and laughed. Janet had heard him laugh once before, but then the danger she faced had come only from the fast water of Pacific Creek. This was infinitely worse, for Dorrity had Patty trapped, and Janet had the feeling that in the old man's fiendish mind some terrible thing was growing. Patty was a Kaywin. Nothing could have suited Dorrity better.

There was no time to go for help. She stepped through the bushes and moved forward smiling. "Patty ran away. I came—"

Dorrity stepped in front of the rocker. "You again! Sit down, miss."

Janet reached past him toward Patty. "Come, Patty. Mamma's waiting."

Dorrity seized her arm, spun her around to sit on the step. She was chillingly conscious of the glitter in his eyes, the purr in his voice, his smile. She had been sure he was "touched," but now she knew he was more than that. He was crazed.

"I'd thought to get all ye Kaywins at one time, but ye've trespassed again, so ye'll stay till I'm through at the hole. The Kaywins have struck it rich at my expense. That diggin' should've been on my place, but they bought that land afore I got here."

She remembered then what Greg had told her on their first ride, that the Government had sold the Kaywins a plot that originally belonged to Dorrity's place. "But what do you think they should have done?" She heard her own voice, a frightened squeak.

"They should've guv it back. It was my land along with this."

"But what can you do about it now? It's done."

"Me?" Dorrity laughed. "I been waitin' an' watchin' fer jist the right minute to blow thet hole an' the Kaywins to smithereens." He snapped his fingers. "With them gone mebbe I could buy my propity back. But this gal tells me the diggin's about finished, so I'll have to deal with 'em now, this minute. All but you two. Ye'll have to wait till I git back."

He grabbed an arm of each and dragged them around the house. There was no fighting his terrible strength. Inside the chicken yard where once he had locked the dogs, he pushed them into the hen house. From the floor where she fell Janet heard him slam the door and push a heavy plank through the slots that locked it.

"Patty!" she sobbed. "Everybody's at the pit. He'll kill them!"

Then she forced the sobs back to help the almost hysterical Patty. "Stop crying, Pat. Listen! Is he gone?"

While Patty listened through her subsiding sobs, Janet studied the hen house, built of inch lumber, its only opening a head-high, narrow, horizontal window on the rear wall. It was screened with chicken wire. Janet snatched up a small, galvanized chicken feeder in a corner and began jamming it against the wire. Sweat streamed down her back and neck, but under her desperate assault a nail finally gave, then another and another all along the base.

Now, how to get out that window? "Patty, can you crouch down and hold me on your shoulders, so I can reach the window? Then I'll pull you up."

Patty held her and from her astride position on the window ledge Janet pulled Patty up and over to the ground outside. "Now, Pat, don't be scared. Just run for home. I've got to go ahead."

Then she skimmed down the meadow to the trail, her

tennis shoes fairly flying until she reached the Two Rivers fence line. She was gasping as she saw him, two blocks away, moving through the timber approaching the pit. In the distance she could see the crowd around the excavation. She tried to scream but her labored voice was a croak in her throat.

He was closer to the pit than she, but maybe she could intercept him. Feeling suddenly spent, she went on running behind the fence line to come in behind him. Her chest hurt, and her throat was dry. So intent was Dorrity that he never saw her coming. He crouched behind bushes less than a hundred feet from the excavation, and for a moment or two he watched the crowd, all of them with their backs to him. Janet could see Martha's blue dress, Greg's plaid shirt.

Then he rose, holding something in one hand while he fumbled at it with the other. As he drew his arm far back, she knew what he had. Dorrity was going to throw a hand grenade into the pit.

Before he released it she hurled herself at him with all her remaining strength. She struck him so hard that she spun him half around, and his arm shot forward throwing the grenade into the timber. There was a terrific explosion

and she saw Dorrity knocked back and down on the ground. She herself was already down, her head wheeling, her ears roaring. Then she knew nothing.

She must have been unconscious only a few moments, for when she opened her eyes Martha was holding her, pulling her away from a tangle of men struggling with Dorrity, who lashed out at them, screaming hoarsely. He flung them off in twos and threes, but finally his terrible strength went and he lay face down on the ground with Burnett sitting on him. Dorrity was limp and wheezing, his hoarse voice babbling. Flecks of foam showed around his mouth.

For the first time she saw Burnett flustered. "Jeff!" he yelled. "Get the sheriff!"

Mid-August had come before Burnett and the Kaywins had everything settled. The silver had been sold to the Government mint at Denver, and the urn had brought more than Burnett had dared to hope. Martha already had picked out some new furniture and a stove. An electrician was wiring the house. The check had come the day before, and Martha and Jeff had discussed its use at the supper table. First, they would pay off the mortgage, and second, money would go into a fund for education for Greg and Patty.

Other things had happened, too. Old Man Dorrity had been committed to an asylum, his case declared hopeless. There had been time this last month to ride, to see more of Jackson Hole. Patty had learned to ride Sawdust, but every time they passed the old cabin on the trail to Pacific Creek, she looked the other way.

"I think," Jeff had remarked when Janet told him about Patty, "that I'll buy that acreage and tear that old cabin down. None of us wants to look at it again."

"Burn that old rocker," Janet reminded him. "Don't forget!"

The first snowstorm of the fall was whirling around the lordly peaks of the Tetons on the day Janet packed to go home. She had just closed her suitcase when Martha came into the room, followed by a long-faced Patty.

"You'll never know, Janet, how your visit took us out of our shells. If it weren't for you, we wouldn't even be here. Will you come again next year? A friend of the Kaywins next time, and not a summer guest?"

"I wouldn't miss it for the world," Janet assured her. She knew that, much as she wanted to go home now, to see her family and start singing again, she was leaving something of herself here, and all through the winter this summer would be something to dream about.

Downstairs Greg made a long, rueful face as he came to take her suitcase. "Now I'll have nobody to tease."

Janet winked at him. "Think of me every time you take Patty riding and play ball."

Greg sighed as Jeff and Martha laughed at him on their way out to the car with her. "I guess I'll have to make that do until next summer."

Famous
Classics

Alice in Wonderland

Fifty Famous Fairy Stories

Little Men

Robinson Crusoe

Five Little Peppers and How They Grew

Treasure Island

The Wonderful Wizard of Oz

The Three Musketeers

Robin Hood

Heidi

Little Women

Black Beauty

Huckleberry Finn

Tom Sawyer

Meet wonderful friends—in the books
that are favorites—year after year

Fiction for Young People

THE RIFLEMAN

THE RESTLESS GUN

WAGON TRAIN

GENE AUTRY
The Ghost Riders

WYATT EARP

GUNSMOKE

ROY ROGERS
The Enchanted Canyon

DALE EVANS
Danger in Crooked Canyon

ROY ROGERS AND DALE EVANS
River of Peril

DRAGNET

BOBBSEY TWINS
Merry Days Indoors and Out
At the Seashore
In the Country

WALTON BOYS
Gold in the Snow
Rapids Ahead

ANNIE OAKLEY
Danger at Diablo
Double Trouble

NOAH CARR, YANKEE FIREBRAND

LEE BAIRD, SON OF DANGER

CIRCUS BOY
Under the Big Top
War on Wheels

HAVE GUN, WILL TRAVEL

MAVERICK

ASSIGNMENT IN SPACE
WITH RIP FOSTER

DONNA PARKER
At Cherrydale
Special Agent
On Her Own

TROY NESBIT'S
MYSTERY ADVENTURES
The Diamond Cave Mystery
Mystery at Rustlers' Fort

RED RYDER
Adventures at Chimney Rock

RIN TIN TIN
Rinty
Call to Danger
The Ghost Wagon Train

FURY
The Mystery at Trappers' Hole

LASSIE
Mystery at Blackberry Bog
The Secret of the Summer
Forbidden Valley

WALT DISNEY
Spin and Marty
Spin and Marty, Trouble at Triple-R

TRIXIE BELDEN
The Gatehouse Mystery
The Red Trailer Mystery
The Mystery off Glen Road
The Mysterious Visitor
Mystery in Arizona

Whitman

Adventure! Mystery! Read these exciting
stories written especially for young readers